The tall, nondesc... watched his target exit the ice-cream store, cone in hand. His target was known to be ruthless—the profile had indicated that he had killed at least twenty women with children in front of their husbands, in an attempt to "inspire" the men to talk. He had to be stopped.

The window-shopper moved. From behind, he threw his left arm around his prey and smashed the ice cream into the man's nose, so he was unable to breathe. His right hand gripped the man's throat, pressing his right thumb against his target's carotid artery. A quick, strong squeeze and the oxygen stopped going to the man's brain. The target slumped to the pavement. To passersby, it looked as if the man had slipped, and the tall man behind him had almost stumbled over him. But instead of helping the fallen—now dying—man, the window-shopper turned into a side street, leaving the sounds of confusion behind him.

Allison Carter, M.D., assassin, disappeared into the boys-and-girls thrift shop to buy a used paperback book.

Assignment complete.

Also by Alexander Court

ACTIVE MEASURES

ACTIVE
PURSUIT

Alexander Court

JOVE BOOKS, NEW YORK

ACTIVE PURSUIT

A Jove Book / published by arrangement with the author

PRINTING HISTORY
Jove edition / May 2002

Copyright © 2002 by S&R Literary, Inc.
Cover art by Ben Perini.

Visit our website at
www.penguinputnam.com

ISBN: 0-515-13298-5

A JOVE BOOK®
Jove Books are published by The Berkley Publishing Group, a division of Penguin Putnam Inc.
375 Hudson Street, New York, New York 10014
JOVE and the "J" design
are trademarks belonging to Penguin Putnam Inc.

PRINTED IN THE UNITED STATES OF AMERICA

10 9 8 7 6 5 4 3 2 1

To the memory of two million Cambodians who lost their lives because one man, Pol Pot, believed in the supremacy of his idea that all traces of western civilization should be eliminated from Cambodia.

To those who were instrumental in the rise and continuing success of Pol Pot's autogenocide: the French imperialists; the Chinese, Cambodian and Vietnamese Communist parties; and the wise men of American foreign policy.

To all the humanitarian world organizations that did nothing to prevent this heinous deed, despite their foreknowledge.

To a world that, even after the well-documented atrocities of the Nazi holocaust, did not seem to care once again.

1

SIEMRÉAB, CAMBODIA

Tourists from all over the world who visit the Angkor Wat temple complex use Siemréab, a small market town five miles away, as their starting point. Like most Southeast Asian towns, be they in Vietnam, Thailand, or Indonesia, poverty reeks through the dust-filled air. Dirty-faced gamins run up begging to any stranger with demands as contradictory and absurd as is the intensity of the dregs of life that they have to endure. "Please, mister. Give me dollar!" "I sell you watch! Rolex. Real, no fake!" "You give me watch! You rich! I poor!" "Here, cold drink! Only one dollar!" "No, sir, don't listen to

him! I sell cold drink for two dollar!" Despite out-
ward appearances, these urchins are anything but
stupid. They are simply repeating words taught
them by their "tutors," usually family members or
older street hustlers.

The stench of poverty these children exude,
however, is real. Unscrubbed faces. Tattered clothing. Bare feet. Their ability to manipulate is impressive in a perverse way. They have learned to
cry, plead, insinuate, beg, steal, and even threaten
the traveling stranger out of a gift. Either by habit
or necessity, they have perfected the technique of
using poverty as a weapon, supported by guilt, hu-
miliation, pain, anger, and the need for retaliation.
The children of Siemréab exist as both the victims
of poverty and its foot soldiers.

This day a group of children were trying to at-
tract the attention of two men walking down the
street, buffered by Cambodian soldiers wearing
green khaki jungle uniforms and sporting automatic
weapons. But the soldiers made little effort to insist
that the children leave the men alone. Insensitivity,
they knew, could arouse the villagers, who would
then accuse the soldiers of brutality and the unnecessary use of force. And no fools be they. With significant numbers of Khmer Rouge soldiers still
wandering about the area, these government soldiers had to be particularly careful of what they did
and how they were perceived. A retaliatory Khmer
Rouge ambush was to be avoided at all costs, including putting up with bothersome street urchins.

Unbeknownst to the thousands of tourists who visited Siemréab and Angkor Wat yearly was the prevalence of Khmer Rouge soldiers hiding in the thick jungle foliage. Contrary to the propaganda of the United States and the Democratic Republic of Cambodia, the Khmer Rouge had neither been routed out by force nor had their leaders been thrown out of power. The simple truth about Cambodia was that it was still in shambles, even after the presumed death of Pol Pot and the much touted "free, uncorrupted" elections supervised by a twenty thousand person, twenty-two country United Nations Peacekeeping Force called UNTAC, organized by the United States. The alleged freely elected democratic government had consisted of King Sihanouk and his number one son, Prince Ranariddh, along with Prime Minister Hun Sen, an ex–Khmer Rouge leader who had been "converted" by the then occupying Vietnamese.

Unfortunately, fifteen years after the war the political situation had not really changed. After forcibly deposing the ineffectual king and the royal prince, Hun Sen anointed himself the undisputed sole leader of "democratic" Cambodia. The warmest part of him was said to be the gleam in his glass eye.

The two men surrounded by the street urchins were well aware of the political situation both within Cambodia and between Cambodia and the United States. The taller of the two, Thomas "Tom" Reed III, a hefty, bald-headed thirty-year career for-

eign service officer (FSO), had been an assistant
secretary of state for several administrations, working in different bureaus. He had now reached the
highest rank a career officer in the State Department could reach—Undersecretary of State for Political Affairs. Reed was now responsible for all of
the regional and political bureaus. He was one of
those few career FSOs who come along once in a
decade, a professional among professionals. According to his peers, he had only two minor irregu-
larities. He was, even by diplomatic standards, a
compulsive talker. He frequently did not know
when to stop talking, which occasionally resulted in
a world leader requesting another interlocutor. The
other problem was his love of his mobile telephone.
He had received unwanted notoriety for having
been the first diplomat to call in reports to State
from the middle of a jungle. Reed had come out of
retirement following a personal request by the president of the United States to accept his current position. So when he met with a representative of
another country, Reed was often considered the
president's personal messenger and not a mere
FSO.

The second man was Sichan Malavy, a short
Cambodian in a clearly expensive suit. Because he
dyed his hair black, he looked significantly younger
than this sixty-seven years. He had a high forehead,
ears that stuck out, thick lips, and eyes that carefully focused on Reed, who was his guest. He rarely
laughed in public, even though he was known to

have a good sense of humor. When asked what he did to earn a living, he smiled politely and responded that he owned several Dunkin' Donuts franchises across America. He was equally proud to say that he was an American citizen, despite the fact that only months before he had been selected to become the new prime minister of Cambodia. The fact of his U.S. citizenship, and his ability to retain it while in the presidency, was one of those mysteries that both a Cambodian desk officer at the State Department and his immediate supervisor, the Assistant Secretary of State for East Asian and Pacific Affairs, would have to ask Tom Reed about. But that was not the kind of question that an undersecretary wanted to answer.

While Reed knew more answers than most, none made him entirely comfortable. Sichan Malavy had been a former high-ranking diplomat, and extremely close to Pol Pot, who was an ardent defender and representative of the heinous former regime. Yet over the last three decades Reed and Malavy had gotten to know one another and, surprisingly, had become close friends through their love of golf. If golf was generally thought to foster comradery, in this case it had forged an unholy alliance as each man tried to enhance the national security of his respective country.

What Reed knew for certain about Malavy was that he was a member of a Cambodian family that had been prominent in the Communist party. Despite the fact that Malavy's emigration to the

United States had been officially protested by both
the International War Crimes Tribunal and the International Commission for Human Rights, he had,
nevertheless, remained and prospered in the States.
He became an important figure in both the Repub-
lican and Democratic parties at the local level in
California, where he lived, allegedly representing
the Asian-American community. He returned to
Cambodia, admittedly reluctantly, at the behest of
the president of the United States, to run as a can-
didate in the so-called "free elections." The president had guaranteed Malavy that he would be a
strong contender. Still, it was quite a surprise when,
only two months before this meeting with Reed, he
had won the election.

The men continued their conversation as they
entered the heavily guarded black limousine. When
they reached Angkor Wat they left the car, followed
by their respective bodyguards, and started to walk
up an impressive avenue lined with balustrades in
the form of serpents.

Angkor Wat, a complex of five temples constructed of sandstone, forms the image of a lotus
bud, the emblem of the Cambodian flag. The
carved, faded reliefs covering the lower gallery de-
pict scenes of daily life and war. The celebrated *ap-
saras*, or dancing ladies, surround the buildings.

The complex was erected during the twelfth century by King Suryavarman II, who dedicated it to
the Hindu god Vishnu. Like all of the major monu-
ments at Angkor, the layout of the temples repre-

sented the entire Hindu and Buddhist universe. The central shrine symbolized Mount Meru, while its gates and cloisters depicted the successive outer reaches of cosmic reality. Moats represented the seven oceans that surrounded Mount Meru.

"It is unfortunate that this is not considered one of the seven wonders of the world," Malavy said as they carefully climbed the uneven and broken steps to the lower terrace.

"Nevertheless, Angkor still represents the richness, power, and prosperity of the Khmer empire," Reed responded as they wandered around the first of three tiers of terraces decorated with statues of Hindu deities and Buddha images, many of which had lost their heads to centuries of thieves.

"Yes, my friend," Malavy interjected, starting up toward the second tier, "but you forget that the construction of Angkor Wat nearly bankrupted the empire. It took thirty years to recover. In the process, we broke with the Hindu gods and adopted Buddhism."

"I hear your message loud and clear." Reed was breathing heavily. "Cambodia is still bankrupt despite all of the money the United States government has given it." As soon as the words left his mouth, Reed knew immediately that he had blundered. This was not the day for recriminations.

The two men climbed the steps to the second tier in an uncomfortable silence.

"This is the perfect place for us to visit together after signing the Southeast Asian Peace Treaty,"

Malavy began, diffusing the tension between them. "I promise you that Cambodia will be a good partner to the others, and a good friend to your president."

"I never had any reason to doubt that," Reed responded, pleased to have had Malavy take the high ground. "Now there is only one remaining problem . . ." Reed stopped, unsure whether Malavy would choose to either acknowledge it or discuss it.

"I would not call it a problem," Malavy interjected. "Your president has promised that before his reelection—which I believe is only three months away—Pol Pot will be returned to Cambodia to stand trial before the people of Cambodia and all the world. The people of Cambodia expect the president of the United States to honor his word." Malavy knew that Reed was smart enough to "hear" the subliminal message: if Pol Pot is not returned soon, Cambodia will embarrass the president by withdrawing from a treaty in which the president had taken great pride—and gained reelection propaganda points—in crafting.

Reed wiped his brow with a sweat-stained handkerchief. "And you are right, my friend. If he said it, then it will happen. You know how it all works. You've been a diplomat. Now a politician." Reed hoped that Malavy was reassured by his words. But he wasn't.

"Your government allowed that manic-depressive French whore to return to my country with his buffoon son—"

"—and look what happened! Hun Sen threw King Sihanouk out and deported Ranariddh upon pretense that he was destabilizing Cambodia."

"That was sheer nonsense!"

"As despicable as Hun Sen might be," Reed replied, "he was the one man who could maintain stability in this country. And you know how much our president and our people want stability in this region."

"Your stock market keeps rising, oil prices are low, food and entertainment are plenty—"

"—and the current unemployment rate is effectively next to zero," Reed finished the litany. "The president wants it kept that way."

"Until the elections, you mean."

"You're not naïve. Americans vote their pocketbooks. The president doesn't want anyone to know anything other than the fact that America is brimming with prosperity."

"Tell me the truth, my friend, why were the Khmer Rouge refugees let into your country? Despite the fact they were mass murderers?"

"Be careful. People in glass houses shouldn't throw stones."

"I do not minimize the fact that I was their controller in the U.S.," Malavy responded, as if that position had wiped his Khmer past clean. "But now that I am here in Cambodia, who will take care of the helpless Cambodian refugees in Boston, New York, and California who are the prey of the Khmer living there?"

"You have no need to worry," Reed responded, unsure whether Malavy was truly concerned or being facetious. "I will make sure that they are protected."

"They will be protected only after Pol Pot has been returned to Cambodia and is in prison." Malavy's thin voice sounded both angry and pleading.

"Although we are using all of our intelligence services, we still do not know where he is. And because of his plastic surgery, no one knows what he looks like."

"But unless you find him quickly, something might happen, and he could die in your country. None of us are getting any younger." Malavy was determined that Reed understand how important this was to him.

"Are you insinuating anything, Sichan?" Reed was indignant. "Didn't our country condemn Pol Pot and the Khmer Rouge for their genocidal activities?"

"Yes, that is true. But that was years ago," Malavy responded. "It made everyone happy, and gave the world the illusion that the 'killing fields' and the Khmer Rouge had finally been terminated." Malavy hoped that Reed was impressed by his English-speaking ability to use a play on words. "And the picture of him being burned?"

"We feel it was pure propaganda by the Khmer, fed to one drunken female reporter who reacted as expected. It received headline coverage across America."

"It is difficult for many Cambodians to believe," Malavy said, purposefully not including himself in his criticism of America, "that Pol Pot has lived so long in your country in anonymity."

Reed decided not to continue the line of conversation. They had followed it many times before to no good end. Malavy would just have to trust both Reed's word and the president's promise.

"Then there is nothing more left for me to do, is there?" Malavy questioned after the short silence.

"Not for the next three months," Reed replied. "Improve your handicap so that we can play a serious round of golf at the Chevy Chase Country Club. That will be your reward for working with me."

"You know they don't accept Asian members, or Jews, or—"

"I promise you that in three months, if everything goes according to plan, and the president is elected, I will make you an honorary member of the Chevy Chase Club."

"And . . . ?"

"If he's still alive," Reed answered in a deliberate tone that Malavy would recognize as ending the conversation once and for all, "he will be sent back to Cambodia."

"You've made me a very happy man. You are both my good friend as well as a friend of Cambodia."

"Don't worry. Just a few months," Reed responded. "I give you my word of honor."

2

WOOD'S HOLE, MASSACHUSETTS

The caravan of cars, recreational vehicles, trucks, bicycles, and people moving toward the ferry destined for Martha's Vineyard was akin to the yearly Muslim hajj to Mecca. Sun worshippers, sailboat devotees, and cynical New York City self-proclaimed intellectuals all waited impatiently in their vehicles or wandered about the Wood's Hole harbor area with the same anticipation and delight as did the faithful Muslims who made the long journey from their respective countries to the holy place in Saudi Arabia.

The Vineyard, as it was known to the "regulars,"

was only forty-five minutes away. And those behemoth boats, given names and ascribed personalities by the islanders, their steel hulls gorging on the influx of vehicles like the big white whale in *Moby Dick* devouring the sea around him, were the means to reach this secular holy land. An island of respite. The summer solstice of rejuvenation. An international playground of sensual abandonment. Only twenty miles long and eight miles wide, each of its five towns accommodated itself to the whims of the vacationer. But unlike the Muslim worshipper, there was no Mohammed to lead them toward spiritual enlightenment. Theirs was completely self-directed, with the only obstacle to fulfillment being the ticket office, for without a reserved day and time for a vehicle to cross the waters, one could never reach nirvana.

Embarkment typically took place without incident. Trucks would be the first vehicles to roll aboard, with the expert aid of a slew of Irish Catholic traffic controllers. Thirty-foot long trailer trucks hauling lumber would maneuver into the ferry, their drivers anxious to board, unload their cargo on the island, and return to the mainland as fast as they could. Once the trucks were aboard, the cars would slowly move up the gangplank, their drivers' eyes riveted to the hand signals of the controllers, attempting to maneuver around the steel underbelly and girders of the ferry without clipping off side mirrors or scratching doors. Overloaded Volvo station wagons laden with bicycles and rub-

ber rafts, and backseats stuffed with children and
bags of groceries, inched their way aboard. The islanders, familiar with the boarding ritual, saw the
maneuvers as part of a well-rehearsed and executed
choreography. The vacationers looked upon the
procedure with a trepidation almost biblical in di-
mension.

Only when the traffic controllers were comfortable with their accomplishments were foot passengers allowed to board and set themselves wherever
they wanted. On sunny, warm days passengers
quickly rushed up to the open, top deck, where they
could begin the tanning process and start to unwind.
On rainy, cold days the creaking leather seats down
below deck were filled with passengers balancing
coffee cups in one hand and the *Vineyard Gazette* in
the other, not even glancing out of the smudged
windows to notice the retreating mainland.

Today, the top deck was complete bedlam. Children ran in and out of the rows of plastic seats while
dogs of all variety chased them, disturbing maiden
voyagers and seasoned islanders alike. Curlicues of
smoke bellowed upward, in concert with the clarion
call of the foghorn announcing that the ferry had
just departed Wood's Hole and was set on its course
toward Martha's Vineyard.

The blue satin waters parted in rolled sheaths of
waves as the ferry scudded across the water. Sea-
gulls flew alongside the boat as if they had been
anointed the Swiss Guard to the Vatican. Their
high-pitched squeals, interpreted as signals of

friendship by the youngsters on board and as signs of hunger by the veteran travelers, were answered by a barrage of food being thrown at the birds by passengers willing to forgo their own hot dogs and popcorn. Once in a while a particularly mischievous child would throw a metal object to the gulls, testing his supremacy over the birds' admirable ability to fly and swoop without any sign of fear. Such children were immediately reprimanded by any adult who might be standing close by; that behavior might be acceptable in a park on the mainland, but certainly not on the way to nirvana.

America had set sail, so to speak, for the Vineyard. The cornucopia of races, religions, and nationalities made the top deck of the ferry look like a boat carrying immigrants to the shores of America past the Statue of Liberty. But instead of clutching a passport, a Bible, or an English dictionary, the denizens of the upper deck held books with the insignia of the National Book Award stamped upon their covers or copies of the latest Sunday *New York Times Magazine* section.

What was not obvious was that the disembarking passengers would immediately disperse to their location of choice according to race, religion, alcoholic proclivity, and social standing. If you were Jewish, and presumably an intellectual from New York City, you proceeded to a modest Cape Cod bungalow of at least three thousand square feet in Vineyard Haven. Those who were darker skinned would enter a waiting car packed with friends and

proceed to the more honky-tonk town of Oak
Bluffs. Those who considered themselves privi-
leged by birth or assignation, and who were wont to
disengage their reared inhibitions with an afternoon—or morning—martini, would proceed in
their Land Rovers, marked by the distinctive rear
window MV decal, to the far end of the island to
Gay Head or Menemsha, towns considered quaint
and restful. To Edgartown went the wealthy, glitz-
loving coupon clippers, unconcerned about anything beyond whether the private yacht club had
received—or denied—any new requests for mem-
bership.

This scenario was simply a backdrop for the tall,
lanky man wearing worn leather moccasins without
socks, who had been on the island for the last three
days. It was early evening as he shuffled along
Main Street in Edgartown, peering into shop windows containing everything from this year's crop of
Vineyard T-shirts, to furniture touted to have been
imported from Thailand, to antique jewelry sold on
commission by islanders unable to accept the unbearable burden of wealth. From a distance the window shopper looked to be simply a "day-tripper,"
one of the thousands of bodies who disembarked
daily during high season for a quick few hours on
the island, only to return to the mainland that same
day.

But on closer inspection one could see that the
window-shopper had a purposeful stare as he
scanned both shop windows and the street and that,

in fact, he was tracking the movements of someone walking a few feet ahead of him. The focus of his gaze was an athletic-looking middle-aged man dressed in a blue polo shirt and beige shorts. The fact that this man was accompanied by what appeared to be his family, however, was troublesome to the window-shopper. Three of the man's children darted in and out of stores while their mother tried to herd them together at each street corner. Their father lagged behind. The window-shopper had not expected to have to deal with his target's family.

Out of habit, the target would occasionally sweep the streets with his gaze to see if anyone was following him. But then he would catch himself in the act and remind himself that he was on vacation, on an island his family had summered on for the past ten years. This was his annual physical and mental separation from the world of work, and the world of the mainland.

"How about some ice cream?" his wife asked the family as they convened on the corner of Main and South Water streets.

"Meet you at Mad Martha's," the kids responded in unison, heading across the street.

"Are you OK?" his wife asked her husband as they followed along. "You seem a bit distracted."

"Not at all," the husband added, a bit too emphatically. "You know, it always takes me a long time to really relax." How could he tell her that the assignment overseas he had just finished had emotionally depleted him? It was not another major acquisition for his investment banking company, as he had told her, but the completion of another assignment for individuals best left unnamed. Memories of his part in the Serbian massacre of the Muslim Bosnians sent chills running through his body on this hot July day. How could he tell any of his family that his business was a front for his being what the world called a soldier of fortune? Since his days in the marines he had been a hired gun, an independent who worked for anyone who paid his extravagant fees.

The window-shopper tried to figure out how he could separate his target from the rest of his family. This was to be his target's final day on the island and his mission was supposed to be accomplished before the evening was over. The assignment he had received was simple. Neutralize the target. Minimize all collateral damage. Unfortunately, the setting was filled with risks he found unacceptable. He had blown two workable moments over the last two days and now he was confronting one of the least desirable settings—a street crowed with passersby and a loving family at the target's side. And he couldn't be sure whether or not his target had a gun tucked in the waistband of his shorts.

The man he was following was known to be ruthless. The profile he had been given at the start of the assignment had indicated that his target had personally killed at least twenty women with children in front of their husbands, in an attempt to "inspire" the men to talk. And after he had been successful and extracted the information he needed, the target had executed the remaining men. Whichever way one looked at his background, the man was a killer, a cold-blooded mercenary who had to be stopped before his next assignment.

The window-shopper watched carefully as the family, children leading the way, walked into the famous ice-cream store. When they exited, ice-cream cones in hand, they headed toward the store with the push/pull toys made of wood. Their mother shrugged her shoulders in enjoyable exasperation. His target lagged behind, licking his dripping scoops of ice cream.

The window-shopper decided it was time—for better or worse. He sped up his pace and came on his target from behind. He threw his left arm around his prey and smashed the ice-cream cone into the man's nose, so he was unable to breathe. His right hand gripping the man's throat, the window-shopper pressed his right thumb against his target's carotid artery. A quick, strong squeeze and the oxygen stopped going into the circle of Willis in the man's brain. The target slumped to the cobblestone pavement.

To passersby it looked as if the man in beige shorts had slipped, or somehow fallen to the ground, and the tall man behind him had almost stumbled over him. But instead of trying to pick up the fallen—now dying—man, the window-shopper turned into the first side street and quickly departed. He left the sounds of confusion behind him.

Allison Carter, M.D., assassin, disappeared into the boys-and-girls thrift shop to buy a used classic paperback book for twenty-five cents. Assignment complete!

3

MARTHA'S VINEYARD, MASSACHUSETTS

Book in hand, Carter walked up Pease's Point Way toward the Captain Cook House of Edgartown. He watched with a perverse satisfaction as a fire engine and ambulance raced by him with flashing red lights and screaming sirens that could have emanated from an Edward Munch painting. But no matter how loud the sirens were or how quickly they arrived at Mad Martha's, there was nothing that these self-anointed saviors of human life could do, except go through an elaborate Kabuki of resuscitation that would elicit nothing but false hopes, astronomical medical bills, and high drama.

Carter's long lean face, hazel bedroom eyes,
wiry body, and delicate long fingers evoked an
image of a Modigliani model lost in a contempla-
tive mood. But he was far from calm. Unlike pre-
vious assignments, he was having difficulty
distancing himself from his actions. Sharp images
of the man's death kept intruding into his thoughts.
Rather than the nineteenth-century homes surrounded by white picket fences, he saw only the
pristine images of a distraught mother and her three
children watch the "assignment" clutch his throat,
gasping for air, as he slowly died in front of their
eyes.

When Carter realized that he was walking across
from one of the oldest cemeteries in America, he
decided to cross the street and walk through the gap
in the fencing. Headstones from the eighteenth and
nineteenth centuries told the history of the country:
sea captains lost in raging storms; babies dying at
birth; families living in death as they lived in life—
together. The newer headstones were more elaborate—they chronicled the death of the island's best
and brightest in World Wars I and II. Several plots
had small American flags set into the ground alongside the marble marker with the distinctive lettering
of the Marine Corps—*Semper Fi*. Always faithful.
What a magnificent concept, Carter thought. Faith-
fulness to God, country, and the specific branch of
the service one was in. What an incredible luxury.
To believe in something greater than oneself and

then dedicate oneself to fulfilling that singular pursuit. That was the American way.

He, too, believed in America—its values, opportunities, and principles of equality—and the one document it was based on, the Constitution. He never ceased to be amazed that men and women were willing to die to preserve that document. And he was proud to be one of those men, carrying his share of the burden. So why did he feel as if his life was fragmented into tiny pieces of ignominy and oblivion? His work was essential to the well-being of the world—to kill those individuals who had committed egregious evil acts and had been officially or unofficially declared criminals by the International War Crimes Tribunal in The Hague, or by the U.S. Criminal Courts. All of his targets had committed acts against humanity. Genocide. Euthanasia. Massacres. Torture. So why did he now feel guilty for the life he had just taken?

Unfortunately, mused Carter, there would be no American flag to drape over his dead body. No medals of distinction and honor for a job well done. For all practical purposes, Carter did not exist to the body politic. He was a virtual assassin, hired and paid for by an American organization that did not exist on either an organizational chart or in a governmental or private firm's budget. Nevertheless, he received payment in seven figures upon completion of an assignment, which he generally donated to the victims of a particular atrocity. In today's case, he would donate his fee to the victims in

Bosnia who had suffered at the hands of the man he had just murdered. There were countless non-governmental organizations, or NGOs, through which he could pass along the money anonymously.

Not unlike the people buried in this cemetery, Carter felt that he had dissolved into some type of ether, to be remembered on occasion and forgotten the rest of the time. He smiled to himself, feeling no other sensation than that of sadness. Perhaps it was the predictable aftermath of assassinating a father in front of his wife and children. Or perhaps it was the beginning of his seriously questioning if anyone really cared what he had been doing for the last twenty years.

Who would remember what he had been or what he had done? The General, his paymaster? The women who he once thought he loved, who he hadn't talked to in years? There were no children to call and apologize to for having forgotten a birthday or anniversary. No living parents to ask about their health—or golf scores. No siblings with whom he could compete. In many ways he was as much a loner as anyone lying beneath one of those tomb-stones.

He had studied enough psychiatry in medical school to have diagnosed himself. The dichotomy between his desire to heal his fellow man and his need to rectify the injustices of life arose from a childhood of emotional isolation in the midst of what should have been a perfect, middle-class life on the upper east side of Manhattan. His father, a managing director of a once successful investment banking house that had gone bankrupt by the time Carter was twelve, was totally consumed by his own business problems and was totally aloof from his son. His mother, a grand hysteric, the stereotypical image of Blanche Dubois in *A Streetcar Named Desire*, could not provide him with emotional sustenance. By the time Carter was fourteen, he had the rude realization that if he wanted to make something of himself he would have to leave the house as soon as it was practical.

His only pleasure during those years of puberty was listening to rock and roll on the radio in order to rebel against his having to study piano at the Juilliard School. While only a few years before, when college students were traveling south to march with the civil rights protesters, Carter was spending his high school weekends in line at the Brooklyn Paramount Theater, arriving at six in the morning, in order to attend that night's rock and roll show hosted by the famous disc jockey Allen Freed. Carter was more than a devotee and less than a groupie. He was, as he would often call himself, a "seriously dedicated rock and roller." Along with this rubric came the expected prerequisites of a ducktail haircut, worn black leather jacket, and argot like "see you later, alligator; after a while, crocodile." Corny by contemporary standards, he thought. But back then it had meant a lot to him. He was part of a group that had a common interest.

To his misfortune, the only scholarship he received for college was one from Columbia University, so that his separation from his family had to wait a few years. He was a pre-med major, hoping one day to become a doctor.

As college ended, the Vietnam War was raging over Southeast Asia. For many white, middle-class young men this period was an opportunity to discover or invent ailments that would allow them to avoid the draft in what was becoming a very unpopular war. For Carter, this was his opportunity to escape his dysfunctional family and become the master of his own destiny. Even if it meant death.

When he enlisted at his local draft board after completing college, the doctors at the induction center were reluctant to accept him because of a documented history of asthma. Refusing to accept a final decision, Carter requested a second physical and was given an appointment three weeks away— enough time, he thought, to prepare himself to pass the physical exam. He remembered spending one entire day at the public library reading extensively on asthma, its physiology, and its correlation to psychological factors. In particular, he was fascinated by the work of a Dr. Medawar, an English physician who had won a Nobel Prize for his work on the correlation between the mind, the immune system, and those diseases which manifest a malfunction in this relationship—in Carter's case, asthma. Medawar had deduced a proposition that would subsequently become the basis of holistic medicine: that the mind-body division was an artificial one.

Carter spent the next few weeks learning techniques to relax his mind and body in the presence of a potential allergen. He discovered that by focusing on different parts of his body he could consciously train them to relax at will. And if his body was relaxed while an allergen, like pollen, was present, he could actually prevent himself from having an asthmatic attack.

Sometimes, good things do happen to those who work hard and are determined. Carter forced himself to relax during his next examination at the induction center and, as he expected, he passed the physical. And for that success he was rewarded, at the age of twenty, with the chance to go directly to Vietnam as a grunt, to serve his country.

His primary task during military service was to flush the Vietcong out of the intricate tunnel networks of Cou Chi. He was nothing more than a "tunnel rat," having to squeeze through tunnels dug for the small frame of the Vietnamese, hugged by walls so close to his body he could barely eat breakfast and still be able to maneuver. Inside the tunnels were pockets of rooms used for different purposes—a hospital room, storeroom, kitchen, conference center. Carter felt like an ant fighting a surrealistic war. One misguided bullet could ricochet through a tunnel or room, and if it didn't kill you, it could permanently damage your eardrums.

To his own surprise, he wasn't at all scared during these anxiety-producing attacks. In fact, he discovered that he had a particular talent for killing. His buddies used to call him "ice man" because he evidenced no fear of dying as he assumed the point position or led his men into what invariably could be an ambush. What his buddies did not realize, but Carter was beginning to notice, was the fact that he was becoming addicted to killing. He liked it. Quite frankly, as he finally had to admit to himself one day, he thrived on it. If he missed a day of field action, he would become irritable, easily exasperated with his companions, and develop insomnia. After trying a cornucopia of legitimate and illicit drugs in order to relax, he finally swore off all of them and decided to accept himself as he was—that he had to confront life and death situations in order to be at peace. So he volunteered for every dangerous assignment, always returning back to base camp with the greatest number of Vietcong ears in his pocket. At the same time, his company commanders noticed that his platoons had the lowest number of deaths and casualties. When he was asked what he thought was the reason, he nonchalantly responded, "I presume that they're more frightened of failing me than encountering the VC," which wasn't either bragging or promoting himself. He was simply stating the truth. Everyone in the command knew that Carter had some lucky aura about him, and if you went out with him on a VC witch-hunt, the likelihood of returning back safely was high.

After two tours of duty Carter used the GI bill to

attend medical school at Columbia Presbyterian Hospital in Manhattan and then joined the Army Medical Corps with the starting rank of captain. After serving several years as a general medical officer (GMO) in Panama, Cambodia, Pakistan, Indonesia, China, and in Fort Meade, Maryland, he retired from the military and became Medical Director for the Department of State, responsible for the medical welfare of personnel in thirty-three different agencies that were housed in overseas embassies, including the FBI, Drug Enforcement Agency, and the Department of Agriculture.

His "extracurricular assignments," as he liked to term them, resulted from many different forces working at the same time. His frustration with the stagnation of institutional systems unable to respond to rogue states or leaders. His own willingness to take on dangerous assignments—for a price. His need to rectify the atrocities that he had committed in Vietnam in the name of national security. Did the ends justify the means? Carter was not into philosophy. But he lived his belief that it was important that someone stopped the evil pervading the world. And that someone might as well be him, a one-man vigilante. And for that he was never apologetic.

A sudden cool breeze abruptly stopped his reverie. He decided that it was time to return to his room at the inn, a charming bed-and-breakfast, owned and managed by a beautiful divorcée who had been married to a physician at one point in her

life. Even if only for a few days, the inn seemed to
provide him with the sense of peace he never
seemed to find elsewhere.

Carter crossed the street from the cemetery,
walked through the garden, up the stairs through the
French doors, and into the nineteenth-century living room. He went over to the credenza and poured
himself a glass of port.

"It's about time you returned, Dr. Carter," the
voice said from behind. "Are you losing your edge?
What if I had a gun in your back?"

4

MANHATTAN, NEW YORK

Richard Sao, a forty-five-year-old, slightly built, well-dressed man hurried from his large west side apartment building, stopping at the red light at the corner of Eighty-fifth Street and West End Avenue. He glanced at his Rolex watch and fretted over the fact that traffic was heavy and that he was going to be late for work. And that would be a poor example to set, since he was the boss.

It was hard for him to believe that twenty-five years had passed since he arrived in the United States as a non-English speaking twenty-year-old who had been fortunate to flee from the war in

Cambodia. Through years of grueling work that most Americans routinely turned down, a dose of good luck, and the greasing of the proper palms, he was now the proud owner of one of the most successful West Coast-Asian restaurants in Manhattan. Like most immigrants, he had worked double shifts, seven days a week. Eventually he built a successful home-improvement business. And when he sold that, he bought two more businesses, both of which allowed him to accumulate a net worth in the seven figures. He had used that money to purchase and upgrade his restaurant. Not bad, he thought. From a straw hut to a four-bedroom co-op apartment. From a rice paddy toiler to the benefactor of a fifteen-member extended family and thirty-five employees.

He looked at his watch again, wondering when the right light would change. These lights, he cursed under his breath, don't understand the commitments of a busy man. He turned around sharply, suddenly realizing that someone might have overheard his words of complaint. Then he reminded himself that he was in America, and here he could say whatever he wanted. But it was hard to erase from his brain the slogan he had heard daily for months in a forced labor camp in the jungles of Cambodia, where he had seen his family and friends killed by the Khmer Rouge: "The organization has eyes like a pineapple."

Sao stepped off the sidewalk and crossed the street as the light turned green, pressed in between a crowd of strangers that had grown around him as he waited on the corner. He walked south on Broadway, glancing at the windows of the world-famous delicatessen, Zabar's. His own restaurant was nearby. And like real estate, a good location was essential in his business.

Sao stopped off at a small international news store owned by a Syrian from Aleppo who had emigrated to America ten years before but still retained a thick accent. Late or not, this stop was a daily ritual that was necessary for Sao's spiritual stability. As far as Sao was concerned, it was important to maintain one's roots by keeping informed of daily events that occurred in one's former country.

The store Sao entered was miniscule, cluttered with newspapers from all over the world. China. Africa. Southeast Asia. Israel. Ahmed was proud of his Syrian origins. But he was equally proud that he was also now an American citizen whose children had graduated from the city's finest university—City University of New York.

"Good morning, Ahmed," Sao shouted at the partially deaf, black-haired man who was busy calculating his morning's receipts.

"*Salaam Aleichem,* Sao," Ahmed said, "you look fine this beautiful morning. But if I might add, you appear somewhat tired."

"*Aleichem Salaam,* Ahmed," Sao replied. "Thank you for your concern. As usual, you are right. I have too many problems in my head. Sometimes I wish I had never started the restaurant."

"Oh, don't even think that way," Ahmed responded, bringing Sao an espresso. "You just need good Middle East coffee to start the day off properly." He poured the aromatic coffee into a demitasse cup and handed it to Sao. "Take one of your papers, read a few lines, and then you will be ready to start a day of work."

"Perhaps you are right, Ahmed," Sao answered. "I've acquired too many American habits, especially hurrying through certain pleasures." He picked up the *Cambodian News*, a daily newspaper widely read by the two hundred thousand Cambodian exiles in the New York City area. The lucky ones. A small percentage of the one-half to one million Cambodians who had been fortunate to have settled legally or illegally in the United States after Pol Pot and his Khmer Rouge cohorts had decimated at least two million of his countrymen, rationalizing the killings with a French-influenced Communist ideology which declared that in order to achieve a truly non-Western civilization, all remnants of western influence must be destroyed.

It was no secret that Pol Pot, Khieu Samphan, Ta Mok, and countless others were the masterminds and executioners of an incredible atrocity. Thirty years later, Pol Pot was alleged to have died a natural death. Khieu Samphan, Ta Mok, and others were ostensibly arrested by the present authorities in Phnom Penh, who themselves had been Khmer Rouge leaders at one time. The former King Sihanouk had "defected" and joined the anti-Khmer Rouge resistance, but everyone knew he was a former collaborator. For Cambodian expatriates living in the United States it was viewed as politics as usual, but they were still skeptical of the official United States position that the Khmer Rouge organization had been destroyed and that all its leaders were either in prison or dead.

"Oh, my God," Sao proclaimed, the cup of coffee shaking in his right hand. "It's not possible!"

"What is wrong?" Ahmed asked, looking up from his calculator.

"This is not possible!" Sao repeated the words in Khmer. "There must be something wrong!"

"What is the problem, my friend?" Ahmed took the cup from Sao's shaking hand and placed it on the counter. His friend seemed paralyzed by fear. "I cannot help you if you don't tell me. What have you read that made you so upset? Nothing can be so terrible if it comes from the printed page. Explosions, earthquakes, deaths in one's family—those are real tragedies."

"Perhaps you are right, Ahmed," Sao responded in a more controlled voice. "Print cannot hurt. Only real people and events can hurt you."

"That's correct, my friend," Ahmed relaxed and smiled. "So please accept my apology."

"For what?" Sao asked, now composed.

"Because the coffee I served you was very, very strong." Ahmed replied, "It clearly had a most toxic effect on your being."

"Thank you, my friend," Sao said, putting both

of his hands together and touching them to his forehead in the customary Cambodian sign of respect.

"May Allah be with you," Ahmed responded. "Don't let the devils within you take over your soul."

"I will remember that, Ahmed," Sao answered. He left the store with the newspaper tucked under his arm, making certain not to disturb the already disheveled stacks of newspapers as he left.

As he walked down Broadway, past the Korean vegetable store, the Russian fish market, and the Spanish take-out for chicken with rice and beans, Sao began to breathe deeply and feel good again that he lived in a neighborhood that was culturally diversified. It made him feel alive. He was part of a community that reflected the real world. Everyone was taught tolerance in school. America was a great country, he concluded. A land where everyone could become whatever they wanted to be without fear of the police or arbitrary violence.

As he came close to his restaurant he noticed a large crowd of people in front of his door. Ah, he thought, this is good for business. The chef must have designed a special dish for lunch and is giving free samples to the passersby. Every time the chef did this Sao saw a marked increase in the number of customers who entered his restaurant that week. Very clever! He reminded himself to give the chef a good bonus at the end of the year.

As Sao insinuated himself through a crowd four people deep, always excusing himself and apologizing for his intrusiveness, he stopped in front of the building that housed his restaurant. Where once there was a beautiful picture of Angkor Wat, Cambodia's famous temple complex, there now remained a large jagged hole in the plate-glass front window. The restaurant had been firebombed.

"I thought we were supposed to believe that they were all gone," Sao said out loud to no one in particular, recalling the headline he had just read, KHMER ROUGE IN AMERICA STAGE ANTI-PEACE TREATY DEMONSTRATIONS. After all this time, he thought, and I am still not free.

5

EDGARTOWN, MARTHA'S VINEYARD

"I'm in no mood for games, James," Carter said, turning to face his colleague and friend, Brigadier General James Atherton, Special Assistant for National Security Affairs in the Office of the Secretary of Defense.

"Then I implore you to finish your port," Atherton responded, disturbed by the distraught look on Carter's face and the tension in his voice.

"When did you get here?" Carter walked over to the sofa in front of the fireplace and sank down into its deep cushions.

"A few minutes ago," Atherton responded, "just

as you—rather sloppily—left that poor man to die an unconscionably painful and, I might add, embarrassing death."

"Are you here to grade me?" Carter asked sarcastically.

"No, I simply thought you might need some companionship."

"Then bring me a dog. At least it's consistent in its loyalty and guaranteed to be friendly." Carter stared icily at his tall, broad-shouldered friend, dressed in a blue sport jacket, khaki pants, argyle socks and Docksiders. From Atherton's waxed moustache and manicured appearance to his effete British mannerisms, Carter had a hard time believing that Atherton had been a poor farmer's son from a small town in Streeter, Illinois. With much work on his part, Atherton had cultivated an Oxfordian accent, mixed with sarcasm, a droll sense of the absurd, and a compulsive need to poke fun at his "employees." Carter knew that Atherton enjoyed the irony that one of his paid assassins was a healer in his public life, having sworn to the Hippocratic oath of "Above all else, do no harm." All in all, Carter found him not only tolerable, but enjoyable to be with.

"Now, now," Atherton responded as soothingly as he could in the affected British accent he had acquired at Andover, the selective private high school he attended on scholarship. "It's clear that you've had a most exhausting night out. Please excuse me for not appearing more sympathetic, but the plane trip from D.C. really fagged me."

"Am I to understand that you are here on an administrative matter?"

"As usual," Atherton answered, looking around the beautifully decorated living room to make certain no one else was present. "Your second payment, upon completion of the assignment, has just been wired to your offshore bank account."

"Thank you."

"No need," Atherton responded. "The business was transacted, as expected. I thank you for a job well done."

"Now, now, James," Carter said, mimicking his friend cruelly, "one moment you berate me for doing a 'sloppy job' and the next minute you can't be grateful enough. So which is it?"

"Haven't you ever heard of Hegel's dialectic?"

"Of course," Carter responded, not really in the mood for the ritual intellectual games that they normally played together. "Thesis, antithesis, synthesis." Given the circumstances, and what Carter knew was a sloppy kill, he sensed a very clear sadistic element to Atherton's challenge.

"Very good, chap," Atherton responded, waving his hand about as if he were conducting an imaginary symphony. "There is no reason for you to feel or possess two contradictory attitudes or achievements."

"All's well that ends well?" Carter asked, relaxing into the comfort of the throw pillows and making a mental note to see about buying some pillows like them for his D.C. apartment.

"Shakespeare was no fool," Atherton responded. "But neither was Freud."

"Freud?" Carter raised his eyebrows. "What does he have to do with my sloppy, but successful assignment?" He finished the port in his glass. Whatever else he thought about this fun-loving overgrown adolescent, Atherton was a former American military hero who now recruited more personnel for clandestine operations than any other military man he knew. Carter, with admiration, would refer to Atherton as the CEO of their company—an officially nonexistent, quasiprivate, quasigovernmental unit informally called the Virtual Assassin Squad (VAS). More often than not, Atherton worked out of the bowels of the Pentagon or Bollings Air Force Base, inside the Defense Intelligence Agency (DIA). But even after a decade of working together, Carter was still unclear about Atherton's current formal position in the established bureaucracy. One thing Carter did suspect, however, was that he, Carter, numbered one of a very few American and foreign mercenaries to whom the General outsourced assignments. As a former chief of paramilitary covert actions for the Department of Defense (DOD), Atherton personally knew individuals with top secret clearances who had completed "wet works" assignments. Rather than wasting their years of training and experience, like the government routinely did with its employees, Atherton had figured out how to enable his contractees to convert vacation time into a profitable second job. Many such contractees were able to retire early from their day jobs by completing only a few assignments for Atherton. Carter was one of those few who decided to remain in his position as Director of the Medical Department at the State Department and work for Atherton when he was on his official time off.

"That brilliant gentleman allowed you, me, and everyone else who has ever made a mistake and felt uncertain about it, to understand their actions."

"What in God's name does a goddamn psycho-analyst have to do with what we were just talking about?" Atherton's mischievous, childish mannerism frequently strained both Carter's patience and credulity. This one man, who was responsible for the tasking of dozens of unofficial U.S. government assassinations around the world, was a character who could only have come straight out of a brilliantly whimsical nineteenth-century children's book like *The Wind in the Willow*, where the characters' madness made them incredibly frustrating, yet exceedingly appealing. Atherton was known among military professionals as the "virtual general," who fought virtual regional conflicts and managed world chaos at a time when formal governmental institutions like the DOD, the CIA, the DIA, and the NSA were being downsized and eviscerated of any effectiveness they might have once had.

"That much-maligned gentleman," Atherton answered, eager to display his knowledge, "contrary to those new Freudian debunkers, is the one person who can best explain your ambivalence."

"Ambivalence?" Carter repeated the word. "What does that have to do with this evening's activities?"

"Facetiousness has gone out of fashion, my dear Carter, just in case you have not heard it yet."

"Oh, come now, James. I'm very tired."

"Did you hesitate this evening?"

"What do you mean?"

"You know exactly what I mean, Dr. Carter."

Silence.

"When else did you hesitate?" Atherton persisted.

"Twice during the week. And then again just before I approached him," Carter said grudgingly.

"What made you hesitate just now?"

"He might have had a nine-millimeter Beretta tucked into his shorts," Carter responded. "But that really didn't worry me," he added. "It was a simple tactical issue which I knew that I could handle." Carter decided to forego his comfort and walk to the credenza to pour himself another glass of port. He purposely took his time, knowing Atherton was waiting impatiently for his response. Drink in hand, Carter motioned to Atherton to follow him out the French doors, into the garden. They sat facing each other at one of the glass-topped tables designed for a memorable breakfast experience.

"It was the fact that he had a wife and three children."

"That bothered you?"

"Wouldn't that bother you?"

"We're not talking about me, Allison."

Carter took a deep breath. "Seeing his wife and children witness their father's death was not something, I realize now, I was prepared to watch."

"But you've done and seen worse. Why did this bother you so much?"

"Ask a shrink that question," Carter responded. "I'm still shaken by the entire experience."

"Precisely." Atherton knew he had cornered Carter. "How would you like to see a shrink, as you so barbarically call the noble professions of psychiatry and psychoanalysis?"

"Are you nuts?"

"Not that I know of," Atherton replied. "But neither do I need the psychiatric training you have had to know that a few glasses of port won't solve your problems. I hate to be the messenger of bad tidings, but for a medically trained individual your insights into yourself—well, they just stink. I fear that you're having problems with your extracurricular profession."

"Oh, come on," Carter stood up and started pacing up and down a walkway lined with flowering hostas, angry that Atherton might have even suggested such a possibility. "What's a psychiatrist going to say to a physician who decides that he would also like to be an assassin?" He paused. "Can you tell me that?"

"No, as a matter of fact," Atherton responded calmly, "I really can't. Nor would I be so presumptuous to assume that I might even venture a conjecture."

"So there you are!"

"What does my ignorance have anything to do with the clear fact that you are having a problem with . . . accomplishing an assignment without feeling guilty or upset?"

"What do you mean . . . ?"

"My dear fellow, before we say things that we may later regret," Atherton interrupted, "let me just make one thing clear. I make assignments. And as you know, I pay extremely well for successfully completing those assignments. Like any decent person, I care about my employees. But as an effective employer, I have to be concerned when my employees' personal problems affect their work. As of this moment, I'm informing you in my role as your employer, that you are exhibiting difficulty in implementing your assignments."

"Are you hinting that if I don't see a psychiatrist I may no longer work for you?" Carter downed his drink in one gulp.

"Let me put it in a more comprehensible, yet I hope more gentle, manner," Atherton said, pulling a piece of paper from the breast pocket of his jacket. "Here is the name of a psychiatrist in whom I have a lot of faith."

"You're not kidding, are you?"

"He's been fully cleared a long time ago. I've sent him several clients over the years."

"So he's an expert in assassins?"

"Not exactly. I would rather like to say that he would not be shocked if the word *assassination* were to arise in the course of your . . . conversations with him."

"I can't believe what I'm hearing." Carter stared at Atherton, incredulous that the doctor was being sent to see a doctor.

"He lives in Brookline, Massachusetts," Atherton continued, ignoring Carter's denial of his problem, "which is only a short taxi ride from Logan Airport."

"This is nuts! You are asking me to talk to a psychiatrist about a world that most people already consider insane. By the way, I'm certain that you never considered the fact I may have trained with him in medical school. And that would make the . . . conversations extremely difficult."

"You have an appointment with him tomorrow at three in the afternoon," Atherton went on. "As a personal favor to me, he will see you. You can talk to him about anything from aardvarks to Zimbabwe. Everything that transpires in his office is kept confidential. I will not know anything about what you say to each other. Furthermore, I really don't care. When he feels that you are ready to return to work, he will inform me. That's all."

"But I'm on vacation from State. I'm booked at this inn for the next three weeks."

"I don't care if you spend them flying back and forth daily!" Atherton's voice was dead serious. "Here are the plane tickets and here is his address."

"And if I don't go . . . ?"

"I'm afraid you don't have the option," Atherton decreed. "It's for your own good. By the way, he trained at Harvard Medical School, the Massachusetts General Hospital, and the Massachusetts Mental Health Center. I believe you trained at Columbia." Atherton started walking toward the garden gate. "Good night, Allison. I encourage you to see him, as your employer and your friend."

"For your information, I also trained with the Uniformed Medical Services in Bethesda, Maryland," Carter shouted at the disappearing figure. He looked at the airplane ticket. The flight was for ten o'clock the next morning.

"And please try to use as few words of profanity as possible," Atherton shouted back. "I would like him to think that I deal with a high class of employees. I would appreciate that very much."

"Certainly, General Atherton," Carter mumbled to himself. "God forbid the shrink should think that he is dealing with one of America's routine, common, death-row killers. That certainly would be déclassé. It would make you just an ordinary hoodlum, contracting out for services to be rendered. If anything is certain, 'ordinary' you are not. And neither am I."

6

BROOKLINE, MASSACHUSETTS

The white clapboard house on Welland Street did not inspire confidence. It looked run-down, unkempt, almost haunted. Carter guessed that the grass had not been cut in weeks. The siding was two years overdue for a paint job. The house was clearly an embarrassment to a neighborhood of expensive, well-maintained homes.

Obviously, thought Carter, our good Doctor Alex Hoffman was desperate for patients. He wondered whether Atherton received a kickback for every patient he referred to him. He wouldn't place Atherton beyond that possibility.

Carter emerged from the taxicab certain that the driver had given him a grand tour of every neighborhood between the airport and Brookline. And the bill reflected the unrequested tour: the sum was $83.25.

As the driver stepped out of the taxi to open the trunk for Carter's luggage, his moon-face brimmed with a cheshire grin. Carter smiled back halfheartedly, recognizing that one of them was going to leave feeling like the biggest shmuck in the world. Either Carter paid the outrageous fare and kept the rage he felt in check, or he gave the driver nothing to have him lose both face and an eagerly anticipated fare.

"Please, sir, eighty-three twenty-five." The driver held out his hand.

"Not in your life," Carter responded, picking up his black overnight bag. "Write it off as the premium for your life insurance policy."

"Premium for life insurance?" The driver repeated the statement questioningly.

"Thank you for the tour of the greater Boston metropolitan area," Carter responded, "but there is no way in hell that I'm paying for your entire day's business." He started to walk across the narrow street toward the doctor's house. Was someone looking through a window, observing what was happening? Carter suspected that it might be Dr. Hoffman. Typical of the sneaky things psychiatrists might do in order to observe behavior, he thought. Then Hoffman would have the gall to ask him to

pay for pronouncements of insight which were
based on nothing more than spying and intuition.

"Please eighty-three twenty-five, now!" the
driver demanded, following Carter across the street.

"Get out of my way!" Carter stared into the
driver's unflinching eyes and sized up his potential
opponent. The man was clearly not frightened of
confrontation. He had probably grown up on the
streets, in poverty, wherever he was born. He did
not look Chinese—too small. And he was too big to
be Japanese. He had to be Southeast Asian—Vietnamese or Cambodian.

"First, eighty-three twenty-five!" The driver attempted to block Carter's path.

"I'll give you fifty dollars, and that's twice what
the fare should be!"

"No bargaining, eighty-three twenty-five! All,
please, or I call the police."

"The police!" Carter repeated. He couldn't be
Vietnamese, Carter decided. Vietnamese love to ne-
gotiate. He must be Cambodian. Only that group
had a strong streak of self-destructiveness. "You
want to call the police. You've got a lot of *cajones*.
Once they see how you ripped me off, it's you and
not me who will go to jail." He knew the driver had
to be bluffing about calling the police.

Carter glanced at his watch, looked up at the
half-hidden face in the window, and decided that
this insignificant incident was costing him a fortune
in lost opportunity with his new shrink. Moreover,
he was becoming exasperated.

"Eighty-three twenty-five. Meter still running. Price go up every minute!" the driver said, parting his feet and bending his knees, as if he were preparing himself for combat.

Carter realized that the driver was trying to provoke him to strike first, so that the driver could take the moral high ground and explain to any authority who might turn up that he was simply protecting himself.

"I have a feeling that you're looking for a fight."

"No fight. Just eighty-three twenty-five now!"

"Please get out of the way."

"Now ninety twenty-five."

Carter then made what was probably his second mistake of the day. The first was to have confirmed the appointment with Hoffman; the second was to swing his bag at the driver, who twirled around with a roundhouse kick that caught Carter right in his gut, knocking him to the ground. Then the driver grabbed Carter's right arm and pulled it upward while he jammed his foot into Carter's right shoulder socket.

"A . . . g . . . g . . . g . . . g . . . g . . . h . . . h . . . h . . . !" Carter screamed, in excruciating pain. The driver knew his martial arts, as if he had been trained professionally. And Carter was becoming too old for this kind of contact sport.

"One hundred dollars!" the driver announced.

"Young man," Carter said, "you've just added extortion to your list of talents." His left hand reached down his right leg and pulled out a snub-nosed Smith & Wesson .357 Magnum. He shoved the gun up the driver's crotch. "This will cost you more than a hundred dollars if you don't release my hand and get the hell off of me!"

"I don't think that Atherton would approve of your methods, Dr. Carter," the driver said matter-of-factly as he released his hold on Carter.

It took Carter a good ten seconds to absorb what the young man had just said in perfect English and another ten seconds to reholster his gun.

The driver offered his hand to help Carter to his feet.

"Don't tell me Atherton sent you to baby-sit me," Carter said, "and make sure I actually made this appointment."

The driver shrugged his shoulders. "Sorry about stiffing you for the fare. But I honestly got lost." He held out his hand. "I sometimes work for the General, as I know you do as well. In fact, you and I and Atherton will be meeting for coffee in Harvard Square after your appointment." He nodded toward the white clapboard house.

"Why should I believe you?" Carter asked, knowing the man should be believed but wanting more assurance.

"Because you know Atherton. He's brilliant. He is playing producer, director, and writer, and we have both given award-winning performances—as he knew we would all along."

Carter couldn't help but to smirk. The young

Asian man had Atherton down cold. Carter shook
the man's hand.

"I will be waiting for you here. After your appointment we'll drive into Cambridge together to
meet Atherton. Only this time you will ride up front
and I will not turn on the meter."

Both men laughed and wondered what Atherton
had in store for them.

As he walked up the steps of the psychiatrist's
house, Carter wondered what Dr. Hoffman had
thought about what he had witnessed from behind
half-closed blinds. Would he have come outside to
help him if Carter had really needed it? Was this
some type of psychological test? Or was the psychiatrist simply afraid of getting hurt?

"Dr. Allison Carter?" Hoffman opened the door
and extended his right hand.

"Dr. Hoffman, I presume," Carter responded,
shaking Hoffman's hand. "I'm sorry that I'm late,
but I seem to have encountered some problems ne-
gotiating a reasonable fee for a taxi from the airport."

"Please come in," Hoffman said, leading the
way through a nicely appointed foyer in his home.
"The taxi should have cost about twenty dollars.
Not much more." He led Carter down a narrow
staircase into a basement office in which there was
the proverbial couch on which the patient could lie
down as well as a chair in which the patient could
sit upright.

"Sit or lie down. Whatever makes you feel comfortable," Hoffman suggested.

"Thank you." Carter looked around the office. Behind the leather couch was an upholstered chair, obviously meant for the doctor. On the other side of the sparsely furnished office was a fish tank which looked as if the water and gravel hadn't been changed for months. The overhead lighting was fluorescent. Cheap bastard, thought Carter. He couldn't spring for some good indirect lighting? An old wooden desk was strewn with all kinds of papers, folders, reports, and pads. Hoffman, Carter concluded, was not into decor.

Carter decided to lie on the couch so that he could recuperate from the blow to his stomach, which still ached. "This feels comfortable. As a matter of fact, it feels so good that I might even fall asleep . . ."

"So that we don't waste very much time," Hoffman interrupted, "General Atherton has already told me a great deal about you. However, I think we should start with my normal intake questions. Family medical history, current medical problems, and the like. As a doctor, yourself, you'll recognize all of the questions."

"Excuse me," Carter sat up, "do you have a wet basement?"

"What do you mean?"

"I mean that your office has a very musty smell—a dampness. Fungi? It's very hard for me to concentrate on anything with that smell permeating everything."

Hoffman smiled knowingly. Carter wasn't going to be easy. But who ever really was? "Okay, we'll dispense with the formalities. How long have you had—some concerns—about your job?" Hoffman ignored Carter's attempt to avoid the issue they both knew was waiting to be addressed.

Carter walked over to a door in the fake wood paneling, which seemed to be an access panel to the pipes. "Take a look here, Doctor, your walls are wet. You probably have termite and foundation problems. And that, in turn, leads to the unbearable smell I was just describing."

"I appreciate your gratis home inspection," Hoffman responded patiently, "but let us not waste time on things which are not helpful to why you are here."

"All right, have it your own way," Carter responded, returning to the chair facing Hoffman's desk. "But would you mind telling me what Atherton told you?"

"Why don't you tell me what you think your problem is."

"I'm not certain." Carter responded almost genuinely, uncertain how much he could trust this bald-headed, paunch-bellied, self-contained, smug man who had not come to his help a few minutes ago. "Do you mind if I ask you a question?"

"Of course not. If that's how you want to begin."

"The first question is about doctor-patient confidentiality. Does it start now?"

"You bet."

"Second question. You stood behind those blinds watching me and the cabdriver come to blows. Yet, you did nothing about it. Why?"

"It didn't look like either of you needed my interference. And my work with you over the next few weeks could have been compromised if I didn't maintain neutrality."

"What do you mean by 'neutrality'?"

"Neutrality means that no matter what happens to my patient in his real life, I need to remain non-interfering and nonjudgmental. This allows me to be more effective in our psychotherapy sessions."

"Let me rephrase what I think I just heard." Carter was incredulous. "If I had been killed in that confrontation with the taxi driver, that would have been of no relevance to you?"

"It would have been as relevant to me as it would have been to any of my neighbors who happened to observe the fight. We all would have called the police."

"But if I managed to get out of the fight with only one arm, one leg, and half my teeth, the only thing that would concern you in this office would be the so-called neutral observations you might make about that particular fight."

"Do I sense hostility to being here, Doctor?" Hoffman knew the direction that the conversation was going and decided not to be drawn into Carter's game.

"You are basically telling me that by maintaining neutrality you are going to be able to help me be more enthusiastic about killing people? And more effective?"

Hoffman thought for a moment and switched gears; better to let Carter vent now, so they could better deal with Carter's hostility later.

"Let me be blunt, Doctor. I'm a contract assassin. I kill bad people for money. And I'm here because Atherton feels that some problems are arising that might make me less effective in my assignments."

"Why do you, a medical doctor, want to be a contract assassin?"

"It pays well?" Carter replied, trying to minimize his sarcasm. He was angry at Atherton for placing him in this embarrassing situation. Now the question was how to extract himself.

"Clearly, that can't be reason enough. You're gambling with your profession, not to mention your life."

"You're right," Carter answered. "But I have my . . . unconscious determinants, as you psychiatrists would call them, that have led me into my dual occupations." The only thing he could think about now was how fast he could leave.

"Which one would you consider to be the most important?"

"The fact that I was a 'tunnel rat' during the Vietnam War and I probably suffered some form of post-traumatic stress disorder." That explanation should suffice for a first visit, Carter decided. It would give Hoffman the feeling he had accomplished something.

Hoffman looked at his watch. "Unfortunately, because of the time taken from our session by your late arrival and your altercation with the taxi driver, our time is up for today. My next patient is due to arrive any minute." Dr. Hoffman stood up, indicating an end to the session. "I know that this was an unexpected beginning for both of us, but since we will be seeing each other daily at three for the next few weeks, we'll make up the time." Hoffman was certain he would never see Carter again. But he was equally certain that one day Carter would have to confront the demons within him.

"I can't thank you enough for your time," Carter responded, relieved. He chuckled to himself as Hoffman led him out the basement door. A psychiatrist's office always had two entrances so that his patients never met. Well, neither of these entrances would see him again.

7

MANHATTAN, NEW YORK

"Mr. Sao, can you think of anyone who might have done this?" Detective Gloria Diaz asked the question perfunctorily, then ordered a uniformed police officer to keep the gawking crowd in front of the half-demolished restaurant moving.

"Yes, ma'am!" the officer responded.

"Yes, Detective Diaz!" she corrected him, taking note of his name. The hell with it, she thought, it's not worth busting his chops. Typical hispanic machoism. She was quite aware that her youth and good looks were as much a handicap in her job as they were an asset. As an extremely attractive

Cuban woman in her mid-thirties, who looked more likely to have wandered out of a boutique on Fifth Avenue than New York City's twenty-fourth police precinct on 106th Street and Amsterdam, it was hard to fit her into the stereotype of a New York City detective, much less the youngest hispanic female ever to attain that rank.

"I can't believe that they would do this!" Sao sat in the passenger seat of the police car, sobbing.

"Please, Mr. Sao," Diaz tried to sound comforting, "you keep saying 'they.' Who are 'they'? You seem to know. And you're afraid of them. Why?" Diaz was sure that Sao's trauma was excessive, even given the firebombing. She had already put in a call for help from Dr. Murray Brown, the police psychologist. But as usual, the gray-haired, wizened therapist was incommunicado when she needed him. He always had some excuse. Usually he claimed that he had lost his pager. Sometimes his cell phone was out of communication range. The hell with him, too, she thought. He wasn't always of much help, anyway. Just a lot of "How do you feel about this?" and "Are there any members of your family who can be supportive?" Once she had discovered that Brown was significantly deaf in both ears, it did not matter what the answers were to his questions. Anyway, she had learned enough psychology at CUNY and at the police academy to guide her through most of a victim's psychological minefields.

"Detective . . ."

"Detective Diaz . . ." She completed Sao's opening, not wanting to embarrass him with loss of memory in his confusion.

"I don't imagine you read Khmer."

"No, I'm afraid not, although I understand a smattering of Chinese and a little Japanese." Oh no, she thought, realizing that she had just fallen in the very trap she hated—that of stereotyping a foreigner, of lumping a Cambodian with another Asian group, even though she knew very well that the groups had nothing in common.

"I did not think so," he smiled back weakly, "I was just trying to lighten the situation for both you and me."

A very nice man, she thought. Unlike most of the ungrateful, entitled victims with whom she had to deal.

"This morning, as usual, I picked up the *Cambodian News* at my friend's newspaper shop . . ." Sao continued slowly.

"Yes, Mr. Sao." She tried to move his story along, as politely as she could.

". . . then I read this passage here." He pointed to a column on the first page. "It's about one of the leaders of the group that killed two million of my people. Maybe you saw the film *The Killing Fields*?"

"Yes, sir, I'm aware of the terrible tragedy that befell your people."

"The leader, Yin Siv, who commanded one of the killing camps, has urged all Cambodians living in

America to support the Khmer Rouge party in both Cambodia and America."

"What does that have to do with the firebombing of your restaurant?" she asked, waving away an approaching uniformed officer. By habit, whenever she interrogated a suspect or questioned a victim, she wanted to do it alone. She needed to get a feel for the flow of the conversation, listening not only to what the person said, but to what was not said. What she was hearing from Sao was that the Khmer Rouge, which the U.S. State Department and the rest of the world had declared "eradicated," was alive and well and thriving, not only in Asia, but more frighteningly, in the United States. How was that possible, she wondered.

"I'm not certain," Sao responded, "but the rest of the article, if I may translate . . ."

"Please go ahead, I didn't mean to interrupt you." She wished he would get to the bottom line— who did this and why? But she mustered the necessary Asian patience.

"Yin Siv, one of the leaders of the Khmer Rouge, categorically denied the common knowledge that the Khmer Rouge had been responsible for the deaths of hundreds of thousands, and possibly more than a million, Cambodians."

"Yes, and . . ."

"Detective Diaz," Sao responded, still shaking, "these men who are staging antipeace treaty demonstrations in your country were responsible for rounding up and killing almost two million of their own people, without even using guns." He paused, hoping that these statistics were as alarming to the detective as they were disgusting to him. "They wanted to save bullets for the larger battle with the Vietnamese, so they simply bashed in heads, and cut throats with knives, scythes, and the rough edges of the palm leaf."

Diaz was somewhat incredulous.

"I have refused in the past to give in to their 'requests' for money. These requests turned into threats, and I, thinking that little could happen to me here in this great country of the United States . . . so powerful. So fair. So democratic . . ."

"What do you think happened?" Diaz interrupted again, not knowing how to speed up this lesson on Cambodian political machinations.

"The Khmer Rouge leaders are very smart. By firebombing my restaurant, one of the more established and successful Cambodian enterprises in New York City, they are sending out a clear message to other Cambodians that they will use any and all means of intimidation to get what they are after in order to control the Cambodian communities in the United States."

"But doing it this way must have very little appeal."

"I wish you were correct, Detective," Sao replied, "but the fact is that while they are detested by people of my generation, the Khmer Rouge have been particularly successful among our children."

"But why?"

"Because they admire the Khmer Rouge rhetoric of needing a strong-willed ruler back in Cambodia and to guide the Cambodians in the United States."

"That sounds like a bit of exaggeration."

"I'm afraid not, Detective Diaz," Sao continued. "The newspaper gives an account of a high school teacher who asked twenty-five Cambodian students whether they supported the Khmer Rouge. How many do you think raised their hands?"

"One, maybe two."

"What about twenty students?" Sao shook his head like a man twenty years older. "It's the same story in Cambodian communities all over the United States. It scares me that our children, born in the United States, having heard from their parents about the horrors of the regime, still support the Khmer Rouge."

"Are you telling me that we are going to have an epidemic of Khmer Rouge atrocities," Diaz looked around at the street filled with shattered glass and a storefront of burnt bricks, "right here in the good old United States of America?"

"That's precisely right, Detective." Sao opened the door of the police car to leave. "You must forgive me. I must arrange all the necessary paperwork for my insurance company."

"Of course, Mr. Sao. Thank you for your time." Diaz handed him her business card. "Please feel free to call me at any time. I will keep you apprised of anything I find out." As Sao started to walk away, the detective had an afterthought. "Would

you like to receive any police protection? To accompany you for the rest of the day?"

"I thank you very much, but I'm afraid it will at-
tract more attention than I need right now."

"I understand." Alone in the cruiser, Diaz took a
cigar from an inside jacket pocket, cut the tip off,
and lit up. It was a Patagonia, a cheap brand that her
cousins had just brought back from Havana, Cuba,
through Cancun, Mexico, after visiting their relatives. She promised herself that when she caught the
thugs who had burned Sao's restaurant she would
smoke the Cohiba they had given her, the most expensive cigar Cuba manufactured. And she vowed
that that time would come soon.

8

CAMBRIDGE, MASSACHUSETTS

As promised, the young Asian man was waiting in the taxi for Carter when he emerged from the house.

"How much are you going to charge me for this taxi ride?" Carter asked as he opened the front door and got in.

"Consider this a free ride." Chev chuckled. For someone claiming no knowledge of the area, Chev drove the battered taxi like a pro through a series of neighborhoods filled with three-decker asbestos-sided houses and oversized recreational vehicles.

"Now that we are almost friends," Carter continued, "what did you say your name is?"

The Asian thought for a minute. "What if I asked you to call me Haing Chev?"

"I would respond that you are too young to be Pol Pot."

"So you know Cambodian history—"

"—for a Caucasian," Carter interrupted.

The young man smiled. "For an American," he corrected. "Most of the people in your country don't even know who Pol Pot is or where Cambodia is located. I'm impressed."

"Now, if I were only on some TV game show . . ."

"You would have won. I don't think many people even in your Pentagon would know Pol Pot's *nom de guerre* was Haing Chev."

"Well, now that you've showered me with garlands," Carter said, "I hope I'm happy to make your acquaintance, Chev. Where are you taking me? To a reduplication of Pol Pot's reeducation centers?"

"Nothing so terrifying. Merely to a coffeehouse in Cambridge where Atherton will be waiting."

They rode in silence for a few minutes.

"I believe that Allison is a girl's name in this country," Chev offered.

"Allison can be both a girl's or a boy's name," Carter responded automatically with a clarification he made at least twice a week.

"Your parents must have wanted you to be quite

strong inside, because many children would have made fun of you as you grew up."

"That's a very astute observation."

"Astute?"

"Astute means sharp, insightful."

"I like that word *astute*. As you can tell, I was not born here. I left Phnom Penh with my parents during the great massacre and we eventually made our way to your country."

"You seem quite proficient in English," Carter noted, "far more proficient than in our earlier meeting today."

"Thank you, but I suffer many limitations. I am completely self-taught because I had to help support my family of seven people and did not have the time to finish school."

"How far did you get in school?"

"Officially, I finished high school."

"How did you do?"

"American schools were like kindergarten for me—I could have learned more from the Discovery Channel."

"Why do you tell me to call you 'Haing Chev,' one of the worst butchers of the twentieth century?"

"Just a bad joke," Chev responded. "But the joke is really on me. That is my name."

"How old are you?" Carter asked. "I suspect you are about twenty . . ."

"Twenty-six. . . ." corrected Chev.

"Whatever . . ." Carter could almost hear Atherton saying "I told you that you were slipping."

"How do you know General Atherton?" Carter asked, and then realized that even if Chev answered the question, he couldn't necessarily believe the answer. "I take that back."

They rode in silence again.

"The General has been good to my community," Chev responded after a few minutes. "There are really very bad Cambodians who came to America illegally during the Vietnamese invasion of Cambodia. They are bad, but they are smart."

"You mean the Khmer Rouge is alive and well and in Boston . . . ?"

". . . and New York, and California, and other places. They have been very successful in . . . organizing support, you might say, for their causes. They pay people a lot of money . . ."

". . . and I bet they ask for a lot in return."

"They give Cambodians some opportunity, but they are also hogs and pigs," Chev responded with anger in his voice. "They claim that they have high overhead—lawyers, bail bondsmen, support for the families of loyal Khmer Rouge." He sneered.

"It sounds like your community is caught between a hard rock, and a harder rock."

Carter and Chev continued to talk about life for both the legal and illegal Cambodian immigrants in the States, and the more they talked, the more comfortable they became with one another. Surprisingly, they agreed on most of the relevant points of Cambodia's history and politics. Where Southeast Asian scholars might differ in their opinions, Carter

and Chev agreed that Cambodian kings had played
off Vietnam against Thailand. They also agreed that
the classical stereotype of the Cambodian as docile
and fearful of change was a myth, probably origi-
nating with the French colonial administration.
While the notion of revolution was historically considered to be alien to the Cambodian character,
Carter and Chev's exchange of dates and events
disproved this thesis.

Cambodia's history, if nothing less, was a time
line replete with revolt and atrocities, starting with
the concentration of power at Angkor in the tenth
century, and the Khmer opposition to the Cham invaders in 1177. This was followed by endless civil
wars and invasions by both sides during the eighteenth century; the rise of nationalism after the de-
feat of the Japanese in 1945; the removal of Prince
Norodom Sihanouk by the Cambodia National Assembly; the Assembly's declaration that the country
was to be a republic; and the invasion of Cambodia
by the Vietnamese Communists in 1974, who over-
threw Sihanouk.

In the 1980's came Pol Pot's autogenocide,
which destroyed or overturned all of Cambodia's
primary institutions, abolishing money, markets,
formal schooling, Buddhist practices, and private
property. The final destruction of Pol Pot's party,
the Democratic Kampuchea (DK), was not far
away.

Most importantly, Carter and Chev agreed that
the precipitant for the rise of the Khmer Rouge, and

the resulting atrocities, was the United States' bombing of Cambodia during the Vietnam War. While the bombings were not the only factor in the rise of the Khmer Rouge—Chinese support, Vietnamese transgression of territory, and the failed attempted CIA-inspired coup by Lon Nol of King Sihanouk were others—they were an important one.

During their discussion, it became evident to both men that an emotional bond had formed between them. While Chev had initially come across as rough and threatening, beneath the scarred, pockmarked face, Carter could imagine a frightened young man who felt the burden of scraping together a living for both himself and his family on a new type of battlefield.

Carter could see why Atherton had engaged the services of this young Asian sitting beside him. The kid was tough. He had learned to survive a life of misery, pain, and torture. He was also a formidable martial arts fighter and a shrewd manipulator. And he had nothing to lose. Carter was beginning to like this young man. He was direct, tough, a high-risk taker, and he was ambitious. He probably could excel at anything he tried, having the kind of drive that comes only from being a grateful immigrant in America. And that's what made this country great, Carter reminded himself.

Chev could barely believe that he was on his way to Harvard. When he was growing up in refugee camps on the southern border of Thailand,

learning to play volleyball from Jay Soloman, a
young American who would subsequently become
a famous journalist and Pulitzer Prize nominee, he
always wore a secondhand T-shirt with bold letters
that read HARVARD UNIVERSITY. When he asked Jay
to tell him about Harvard, he received a two-hour
lecture, including the names of famous world leaders who had graduated from that university. The list
seemed endless, and Chev was appropriately hum-
bled. So heading toward the campus of the epicen-
ter of knowledge and the starting place of powerful
leaders was extraordinarily energizing. For Chev,
knowledge was power. And power was paramount.
It was paramount as he watched members of his
family slaughtered by the Khmer Rouge. It was
paramount when, as a ten-year-old, he participated
in the internecine battles of the Khmer Rouge. Propaganda. Education. Reeducation. All were part of
knowledge . . . and power.

9

MANHATTAN, NEW YORK

"May I please talk to the desk officer for Cambodia?" Detective Diaz requested of the U.S. State Department telephone operator in Washington, D.C. She waited for what seemed an inordinately long time, inured to the chaos that surrounded her as her colleagues shouted back and forth across desks, and suspects taken into custody cursed under their breath as they sat handcuffed in rickety wooden chairs. Just another typical day in New York's twenty-fourth precinct. Diaz thrived on the vitality in that room, even if political correctness and gender sensitivity training had gone the way of the wagon train. "Hello, is there anyone there? I've been on hold for ten minutes!" No one answered. "So much for our federal government and its accessibility to the public," she muttered to no one in particular.

"Hey, Diaz," an Afro-American policeman called to her as he walked by her desk. "I've never seen you wait so long on the phone for anyone or anything. Usually you would have cut the person making you wait a new asshole."

"Thank you for your supportive observation." Diaz smiled, raising her middle finger and slipping him an eagle.

"Now I recognize our old familiar Diaz." He laughed. "Certainly wouldn't want you to change from your old sweet self."

"You wish, honey! In your dreams!" She placed her feet on her desk and tipped her chair back.

"What can I do for you?" a voice on the other end of the telephone suddenly asked.

"I'm Detective Gloria Diaz from the twenty-fourth police precinct in Manhattan." She resented having to feel grateful for having someone finally talk to her. "I'd like your name and title, please, so I know if I've reached the right person." She found it strange that the State Department official did not identify himself when he answered the telephone.

"My name is John Doe and I'm a political officer on the Cambodia desk."

"John Doe? That's a name we use as an alias

when we don't want the real identity of a person known."

"Detective Diaz," Doe retorted, "we do the same thing. We get a lot of crank and threatening calls. It's part of our security procedure. I think you can appreciate that."

"Do I have a choice?" she asked, deciding that she would not like Mr. Doe if she ever met him.

"I don't think so," Doe answered politely. "How may I help you, Detective?"

"Just for curiosity sake, how do you know that I'm really a detective calling from Manhattan?"

"Normally, we wouldn't answer that question. But while you were on hold, I traced the location of the call and checked with your supervisor to determine whether there was a Detective Gloria Diaz. With all due respect, they gave a resounding affirmation to both your existence and ability. So, even though I must maintain my anonymity, I have been instructed by my supervisor to help you in any way possible."

"Well, it's good to know that the federal government is . . . so concerned with disseminating sensitive information in a discreet manner." Horseshit, she thought, this is the most convoluted system of mistrust that she had encountered in a long time. And why would a State Department official have to retain anonymity? Maybe an intelligence operative at the CIA, DIA, NSA, or NRO would have to assume the ridiculous identity of John Doe. If she pulled that crap. . . . Fuck it, she decided. Every system has its own Kabuki. Who the hell was she to question why or what the State Department was doing? All she had to do was listen to what John Doe had to say and assess its value. As her captain would often tell her, she had to put a cap on her carburetor.

"We appreciate your understanding, Detective Diaz."

"Let me get to the point. I responded to a crime scene today where a restaurant owned by a Cambodian was firebombed—"

"Was this on Broadway, in the low eighties?" the voice interrupted.

"Yes, how did you know?"

"We've been tracking a group of professional arsonists, most likely Cambodian born, who have been extorting wealthy Cambodian businessmen for the purpose of extracting money to support their political group."

"What's the name of the group?" Diaz wondered how much the State Department officials really knew . . . or were willing to say.

"Richard Sao may have told you that they are called the Khmer Rouge."

"How did you know about Richard Sao?"

"That's classified, ma'am. I'm afraid I'm not allowed to tell you."

"Clearly, you and your people seem to be on top of these Khmer Rouge types. How do you know all this?"

"Part of it is classified. But, I can tell you that

we've been using ELINT, HUMINT and other forms of intelligence to track the behavior of the Khmer operatives. We have no choice."

"What do you mean?"

"Many Khmer Rouge came to the United States in 1979 when the Vietnamese invaded Cambodia, drove them to the border of Thailand, and almost destroyed them."

"How did we let that happen?"

"I'm afraid that's classified information."

"A security issue again?" Now she was sure that she didn't like the man behind the voice. She took out a Patagonia and clipped its end off. She wondered what sex would be like with such a tight-assed, paranoid gringo. The woman probably wouldn't know when she was penetrated because that would be classified, too.

"To tell you the truth, I'm really not certain. It occurred before my time, during the Carter administration. Whatever happened occurred at a senior level. I'm not privy to the record of those deliberations. I have no idea who allowed the flood of Khmer Rouge immigrants to come into the U.S."

"Are you trying to tell me that some high government officials made the decision to let the leaders of the Khmer Rouge in, despite the fact that they did some pretty bad shit? I mean—"

"That's okay, Detective, I've heard and said worse. Your statement is right on the mark. That's why we knew about the firebombing on Broadway. We track as many of the Khmer leaders as we can.

But it's been very hard to pin anything on them. They've bought a lot of congressional protection which, of course, comes into play the closer we come to apprehending anyone for a crime."

"This sounds like one big gang bang of multiple interests."

"That's one way of summarizing it. Speaking on my own behalf, and not as a U.S. government employee, you would be doing a great service to mankind if you could apprehend the individuals responsible for the firebombing. The Department of Justice might even be persuaded to hand out medals—"

"I hear you loud and clear."

"Now forget everything I just told you. It was never said."

"What was it that we were talking about, anyway? Oh yes, what do you know about this group?"

"Before today's firebombing there were smaller episodes of intimidation, vandalism, extortion, and corruption. But today's incident indicates that the Khmer are escalating their level of violence."

"Who is running the operation here in New York?" She was going to ask him what *ELINT* and *HUMINT* meant, but she did not want to sound stupid. "Clearly, all kind of intelligence is being used to track these guys, so why haven't you been able to catch anyone?"

"You could probably answer the question better than I. It's all a question of inducing scared victims to testify against perpetrators who they know will eventually kill them if they go to the police. We haven't been able to establish a direct link between any one incident and direct orders from Khmer leaders."

"The same old problems we had in the past with the Italian Mafia. So can't we get these guys on a RICO charge, a conspiracy to commit a crime?"

"If you can trace this firebombing directly to one individual, and you can find out where his instructions came from, and then you are able to convince Mr. Sao to testify against him, or them, and convince the firebombers to turn against their own bosses, then, and only then, we may have a RICO case. I hate to put it this way, but you are our best chance of apprehending these war criminals and their young protégés."

"With all the billions we spend on intelligence and national security, you're telling me that the entire case depends on one Cuban-born detective working the streets of New York City?"

"Yes, ma'am."

"Please, don't call me ma'am. It makes me feel old."

"Yes, Detective."

"That sounds about right. If you don't mind getting to the bottom line, could you give me a name of some 'bad guy' in this area?"

"Be happy to, Detective. And if you are able to apprehend this man with evidence strong enough to convict him, then you may just get to be a genuine American heroine."

"Thank you, Mr. John Doe." Unclear whether she should be facetious or serious, Diaz decided to take the middle ground. "On behalf of my precinct and myself, I would be more than honored to help my government." If anyone in the precinct had heard her, they would have barfed. But what did it hurt her to say what Doe wanted to hear? For her, whoever this scumbag Cambodian was, it was just another killer she had to collar.

"The man you want is Sonn Senn, publisher and editor-in-chief of *The Cambodian News*, located at Forty-third Street and Broadway. On the surface he's sweet, pleasant, and polite. But we've lost several operatives who went after him. In short, he is a ruthless killer who will stop at nothing to eradicate someone."

"Thanks for the warning, Mr. John Doe. Even though we Cubans love to rumba and mambo all night long, piss us off and see what happens. Castro isn't the longest living dictator in the world for nothing." She took a long drag on her cigar and blew the smoke into the air as she hung up the phone.

10

CAMBRIDGE, MASSACHUSETTS

The coffeehouse into which Carter and Chev walked reminded Carter of his own college days and the countless hours spent discussing Kant, Hegel, Schopenhauer and their influence on Nietzsche's concept of the will. But those were the days when studying philosophy, if not a luxury, was at least an indication of aspired to culture. Today's students, sipping their lattes over spreadsheets, were digesting tomes by Warren Buffet and Bill Gates, the new philosopher-kings.

Atherton greeted them both warmly, as if it was a scheduled meeting which each had carried around in his respective appointment book or Palm Pilot. He had already consumed two espressos and had heard from Dr. Hoffman that the likelihood of Carter returning for therapy anytime soon was nil to nonexistent. So much for arranged *shitachs,* Atherton thought, pleased with his use of a Yiddish word, one of many he had learned when stationed in Israel for four years.

The waiter came over and took their orders.

"I'm glad you two have finally met," Atherton started off, as if their meeting earlier in Brookline was the typical luncheon at The Plaza. "I thought you both would get along famously."

"I'm not sure that *famously* is the operative word, so to speak," Carter responded, "but if you mean will we be able to work together, I think that the answer is yes. Once again, General, your instincts were correct."

"For a few minutes this morning I thought that I would not live to be part of this meeting," Chev said with a smile on his face. He turned to Carter, "where were you when my country needed you years ago?" he asked rhetorically.

The men remained in silence as the waiter, most probably a struggling graduate student at one of the universities in the Boston area, brought them their drinks. Students at nearby tables were now being served sprout sandwiches and quiche; the late afternoon hour was slipping toward vegetarian dinners for the incoming patrons.

"So, what is the verdict?" Atherton continued

once they were alone. "I need both of you to be closer than a tight end, as you football fans say. The long and the short of it is that if we don't identify and . . . neutralize . . . Pol Pot before the election, I might as well check out my retirement benefits. He will destroy the treaty that the president has just signed, support the agitation of his followers here and in Cambodia, and create an atmosphere of instability in Cambodia that may just lose the reelection for our current owner and master."

Chev remained silent. He knew why he was at this meeting. His entire life had been geared for revenge. But the assignment was new to Carter, and the look on his face told Chev that he had lots of questions.

"Why me?" Carter began.

"Aside from what Hoffman had to say, we both know you're one of my best. And your target is so . . . you'll get a great satisfaction out of completing this assignment."

"Perhaps I should ask, why me?" Chev interrupted, just so Carter wouldn't feel that this pairing of the two of them wasn't an unreasonable assignment for a loner.

"First, our CIA haven't come up with squat. Second, none of them are Cambodian. While any Asian agent might be able to confuse a few self-important journalists, they wouldn't make any headway infiltrating the Cambodian community. And you have a big head start already." Atherton paused, hoping he need not have to repeat the obvious again. "A done deal?"

Carter turned to Chev. "Can Atherton and I have a few minutes alone?"

Chev decided that he had some telephone calls to make and left the two men staring at each other.

"I want you to work with Haing Chev. If he needs assistance, I want you to help him. You both know what the assignment is."

"Even if that means additional assassinations?"

"Especially if that means additional assassinations. He certainly doesn't need tips from you on how to cure a duodenal ulcer." Atherton paused and tried to inject some humor into what might become a 'situation.' "Although I might."

"Arrangements?" Carter responded in businesslike fashion, ignoring the friendly tone.

"As usual. Seven figures, beginning with five—"

"No," Carter interrupted, "this time we are going to begin with seven."

"Why?" Atherton asked. "You have a partner! In fact, I should probably cut it in half."

"It's because I have a so-called partner that I'm adding two million to the price. You know that I always work alone. As far as I'm concerned, he's not an asset and possibly a detriment."

"I'll split the difference in half and give you one million more."

"Acceptable!"

"Then it will be wired to your offshore bank. I believe you've changed it from the Cayman Islands to Liechtenstein. Is that correct?" Atherton felt comfortable again. Business was business.

"You know damn well that it is! You just wired funds for the Vineyard assignment. So stop playing games with me, General!"

"Then we are agreed."

"The deposits are to be redistributed to my usual favorite charities. And you better be able to cover me at State."

"Oh, by the way, before I forget," Atherton tried to sound as if an innocent afterthought had suddenly come into his head, "this assignment has another small component. Nothing major."

"Are you asking me for a twofer?" Carter was suspicious of Atherton's tone of voice.

"I consider that question a bit crass, Dr. Carter," Atherton responded, assuming the posture of having been insulted. "It's really quite simple. Nothing very complicated. While I want you to help our friend—"

"—you want me to finish the assignment by making certain that our friend can't bear witness against us?"

"A correct deduction. Let us just say that after your assignment is completed, there will be no people or evidence that could trace us to anything."

"Whom are you protecting?"

"Yes or no, Dr. Carter?"

"You already know the answer."

"Communications between the three of us will be kept at a minimum. Preferably, none, until you've completed the assignment. Give yourselves one month—not more. I don't want our higher authorities to start getting nervous at election time. But I also don't want so much time to go by that your target surfaces and does damage to our country like he did to Cambodia."

"Are you going to wish us—me, good luck?"

"Luck is a matter of taking the wrong plane," Atherton responded, "the rest is professionalism."

11

Detective Gloria Diaz sprinted down Broadway as if she were going to meet her lover, a Jamaican doctor who worked in the emergency room of Roosevelt Hospital. At this moment in her life, Diaz was very much in love. And for her that was quite a feat. Several serious boyfriends. Several serious failures. Or more aptly, several serious disasters. She was grateful to finally have someone in her life who was not threatened by her intensity, intelligence, and passion.

P. J. Allen, M.D., was a tall, lithe, dark-skinned man whose very movements made her quiver with

anticipatory excitement. On their recent vacation in
Havana, Cuba, illegally bypassing the official U.S.
embargo by entering from Jamaica, they had spent
all their waking hours either making love or dancing on the terrace of the Hotel Nacional. Allen had
not been intimidated when Diaz informed him,
matter-of-factly, that she had not been sexually sat-
isfied by his lovemaking. Instead, he had broken
out into a deep-throated raucous laughter, declar-
ing, "Woman, you have more sweet juice in you
than any mango I have ever eaten. Let's try again!"

But now those piquant memories of color and
movement and song had to be put on hold as Diaz
stood in front of the narrow rundown building on
the south side of Broadway and Forty-third Street.
The stenciled numbers on the building were faded.
The remaining gold letters read something like
ROSE . . . G BUIL . . . G. According to the directory
attached to the brick exterior, the building was filled
with a series of small offices. Law firms. Export-
import companies. Computer start-ups.

She wondered how easy it would be to walk into
one of those computer start-ups, offer her services
to do . . . anything . . . receive her options and become one of those hotshot millionaires. That was
something her family would certainly boast about.
Unfortunately, the only thing she loved more than
Allen right now was her job. And she wouldn't
trade that for any amount of money.

The rush of adrenaline that accompanied her
walk up four flights of stairs wasn't enough to mask

the fact that she was almost out of breath. Clearly, she had to work out more consistently. For a while she had used the police gym, but soon grew tired of the taunts of the guys. They were right, she would rather smoke a Patagonia than spend an hour with a treadmill and free weights. But given her labored breathing by the time she stood on the landing of the fourth floor, Diaz decided that she would have to be content with chasing an offender in a squad car—or shooting him. It would be a lot more effective than trying to apprehend him by foot.

The entrance to the *Cambodian News* was singularly unimpressive. The once-bold black lettering on the nicked and scratched mahogany door to the office was faded. The marble floor in the hallway, an important leasing attraction ninety years earlier, was now dirty and stained. The faint smell of urea lingered in the air. Despite the fact that this was the headquarters of a major ethnic minority newspaper, Diaz thought, there was a moribund quality about it, starting from its very entrance.

When Diaz opened the door she entered a sparsely furnished office. Three aluminum tables that were being used as makeshift desks, with a half-dozen folding chairs, crowded together along a wall with two dirty, cracked windows. Paint chipped from the walls. Install-it-yourself tiles were popping up from the floor. There was no frenzy of activity, no workers walking hurriedly about because of a journalistic deadline. Her investigative nose told her very quickly that this office was a front for something. But not a newspaper.

A woman with a large scar down the length of her cheek was seated on one of the folding chairs, hunched over papers on one of the "desks." She didn't bother to raise her head to look at Diaz as she stood in front of her.

"Excuse me, ma'am, could you tell me where I could find Mr. Sonn Senn?"

"Not here!" the old lady muttered, scarcely acknowledging Diaz's presence.

"I was told that he would be here," Diaz responded harshly, sensing that this woman was lying.

"You wait!"

"For how long?"

"Just wait!"

"I'm Detective Gloria Diaz and I am here to question Mr. Sonn Senn!" She raised her voice this time as if the old lady was deaf. Subtlety was quickly buried by mounting impatience. If righteous indignation did not work, she would probably have to resort to verbal threat, followed by physical intimidation. By one means or another, Diaz would have her questions answered.

"Please wait! He's not here!"

"Where is he?" Diaz demanded, now curious why the woman still hadn't raised her head up once to look at her. Could she be ashamed of the scar? Shy? Or was she simply telling her the truth, that

Sonn Senn was not there, and that ended all discussion?

Diaz looked around the room. Why was no one else present, she wondered. The tabletops were as empty as the four walls. Computers? Typewriters? Personnel? There was a scratched wooden door to her left and Diaz started walking toward it.

"Don't open!"

"Why?"

"No one allowed!"

"That's just what I wanted to hear." Diaz tried to turn the doorknob, but it didn't budge.

"Closed! Only for officials!"

"Lady, I'm an official of the law!" Diaz answered, walking back to the old woman, "And I'm going in there because I have the legal right!"

"You have no legal right!"

"I have probable cause to think that . . . something illegal may be going on in this office," Diaz lied, assuming the woman didn't know anything about American law enforcement.

"Only your imagination! Nothing happen here, except newspaper!"

"Before I bust open that door, lady, tell me where Mr. Sonn Senn is."

"No one here!"

"You are here! And who are you?" Diaz unbuttoned her jacket so that her .38 Smith & Wesson was readily accessible. "Silence is a perfect cover for violence," was a popular axiom around the

twenty-fourth precinct, and Diaz was a true believer.

"No one! Just work here arranging papers!"

"Do you mind if I see what you do?"

"Please go! Nothing to see here! No Mr. Sonn
Senn. No work to see!"

"I don't understand why you would object to my
seeing what you do."

"Do nothing of interest to Detective Diaz!" The
old lady slouched further down as Diaz walked
around the desk. By this time, Diaz's right hand
was wrapped around the black handle of her gun,
ready to draw and fire at a moment's notice. But the
more closely she scrutinized the old lady, the more
Diaz was convinced that there was something
strange about her. For one thing, she had very little
hair. And although slim, she had broad shoulders.

"Please put your hands up in the air!"

"Can't put hands up!"

"Why?"

"Terrible disease, arthritis!"

"I'll say it just one more time. Put your hands up
in the air!"

For the first time, the old lady sat back in her chair
and looked at Diaz as if she were taking her mea-
surements. She took a long time to speak. "I'm Sonn
Senn, Detective Diaz!" The old "lady" stood up
straight, standing barely five foot four inches tall.
"We Cambodians are gentle people who are sometimes seen as being vicious. I am simply making certain that my enemies, who might gain access to my

office, do not try to kill me. So I assume the disguise of an old woman. As you can see, it is not hard for an elderly Cambodian man, with what you Americans would call 'effete' mannerisms, to assume that disguise."

"What enemies would you have?"

"As editor-in-chief of a controversial newspaper, can you not imagine how many would like to find me and inflict some sort of pain for real or imagined insults?"

"Aren't you overreacting a bit?" Diaz reholstered her revolver and snapped the leather strap closed to secure it.

"I'll leave that up to you to judge!"

"What do you mean?"

"Suppose someone threatened your life and family for printing the truth. What would you say to that?"

"In principle, I would say that you should have called the police."

"The American police are very good at what they do, but we Cambodians have our own particular course of justice that doesn't often correspond to your laws. We tend to be highly emotional people. Gentle and soft, but combined with a ferocity can result in . . . killing fields." Sonn Senn stopped speaking abruptly, as if he decided not to bring up an unpleasant memory.

"You don't seem to have any workers. Are you a one-man newspaper?" Diaz ignored the reference to killing fields, but remembered that Richard Sao had also brought it up in conversation.

"On the contrary," Sonn Senn laughed. "We tend to be quite busy. But this morning we received a death threat. I made the decision to evacuate the office, leaving only myself here."

"That's very noble, Mr. Senn." Diaz paused, reflecting on words that sounded too self-righteous, even unctuous. "But who threatened you and your employees?"

"A very dangerous man. A former Khmer Rouge camp commander."

"And what kind of threat did this man make?"

"He threatened to kill everyone in this office."

"Why?"

"He claims that I am responsible for firebombing his restaurant."

"What is his name?"

"He goes by the anglicized name of Richard Sao. His real name is Lon Nol. A monster who personally killed over ten thousand Cambodians without the use of one single bullet."

12

Carter and Chev exited the Red Line station at Fenway Park in the rundown Roxbury neighborhood of Boston. They were on their way to Chev's community, where he wanted to introduce his American colleague to some of his Cambodian buddies.

"This neighborhood hasn't changed in the past twenty years," Carter said, noticing five black teenagers congregating around a liquor store drinking whiskey from bottles covered by brown paper bags. He had spent several months during his medical residency training detailed by the army to a Boston hospital. The liquor store, like most of the stores in the neighborhood, had a roll-down metal security grate on both sides of the entry, sprayed with colorful graffiti. A wrought-iron gate secured the beat-up wooden front door. Garbage littered the sidewalk and streets. Several nondescript cars sat without hubcaps and wheels. Carter felt the hostility of the black teenagers even before he and Chev passed them and heard the catcalls.

"How do you like my neighborhood?" Chev asked rhetorically. He pointed to the group of teenagers. "That's the trash that's hardest to get rid of," he shouted out.

"What did you say?" Jason, a tall, stocky, nineteen-year-old who was the designated leader of the group shouted back. His words were drowned out by the shouts of profanity rising like a gospel choir from his friends, all of whom started to approach Chev and Carter.

"I told my friend here that you and your asshole buddies are nothing but trash that has to be thrown out and burned," Chev said coldly. He knew he was being provocative, but he wanted to demonstrate to Carter how he was able to handle these bullies who had continuously tried to instigate fights with him and his Cambodian friends since they moved into the neighborhood five years ago.

"I hope you know what you are doing," Carter whispered, concerned by the obviously impending melee.

"Don't worry, man," Chev quietly assured him.

He turned to the teens. "It's punks like you who are crapping up this neighborhood . . ."

"Okay guys, let's break it up!" Carter interjected, watching Jason's eyes in order to assess whether he was about to reach for a hidden weapon. Carter patted his shoulder holster to reassure himself that "old reliable" was still there. But it would be very messy if he had to use his .357 Magnum Smith & Wesson against these young hoodlums. How could he justify it? This type of action was certainly not part of his assignment. And he was already on Atherton's shit list. He would have a very hard time trying to explain to him how maiming or killing five black teenagers was in any way related to finding Pol Pot.

"Hey, kimchi breath, is this honky your father?" Jason taunted, pointing to Carter. "How did you get hooked up with him? Your mommy suckee, fuckee white bread here?"

"No, actually he told me that your mother had a bargain sale a couple of months ago and she serviced him while she was cleaning his toilets."

Carter grimaced at the insult. As the gang members approached, it reminded Carter of his childhood attending Booker T. Washington High School some thirty years before, where the white students were definitely in the minority, and even basketball games in the park ended with his being thrown off the court and chased down the streets of New York City, until he relinquished the ball—forever.

"Now, would you mind getting out of the way so that my friends and I can pass by without having

any of that black dirt rub off on us," Chev continued, clearly looking for a confrontation.

"Listen, Chink, get out of our neighborhood before it's too late," Jason threatened.

"I'm Cambodian, not Chinese, stupid."

"Chinese, Cambodian, that's all the same to me."
Jason laughed.

"That's what I figured. So it's true what they
say . . ." Chev was escalating the confrontation
quickly.

"Yeah, man, what would be that?"

". . . that there is no difference between you and
a monkey," Chev responded.

"You're calling me a monkey?" Jason asked.

"Yeah! What are you going to do about that?"
Chev responded.

"Okay, everyone, let's cool down before it gets
out of control." Carter placed himself between
Chev and Jason, once again astonished to see how
little had changed when it came to prejudice and
stereotyping.

"Hey doughboy, get out of my face!" Jason addressed Carter as he reached for a switchblade in
his pants pocket. "The Chink and I don't need any
United Nations between us."

"Don't fuck with The Man," Chev said, egging
on Jason even further. By designating Carter as The
Man, Chev had set Carter up as a convenient flash
point for Jason.

As Jason whipped out his knife and snapped it
open, Carter thrust his right thumb above Jason's

left orbital bone, just at the point at which the fifth trigeminal nerve exposed itself and then passed through the eye orbit to reenter the skull. He pressed on the nerve, hard.

"Ag...g...g....g...h...h...h...h...h!" Jason screamed as he started to sink to the ground, desperately holding on to the knife as his last point of dignity.

"I suggest you release that knife," Carter whispered in his ear. "I can assure you that I would be only too happy to inflict more pain."

"I give up, man," Jason shouted from the sidewalk. He released his knife on to the pavement. "Man, that shit really hurts!"

"Get up!" Carter ordered, carefully watching the movements of the other four teens. "I want you to apologize to my friend for your boorish behavior."

"I'm sorry for what I said." Jason rubbed his face with his fingertips to try to make the pain go away.

"Now promise that there will be no more harassment of anyone who is Asian."

Jason hesitated long enough for Carter to grab both Jason's wrists.

"I promise. I promise," Jason shouted, "no more dissing of anyone, especially the Chinks."

"The correct word to describe Chev and his friends is *Cambodian*. Not *Chinks* . . ."

"OK, OK, not Chinks, but Cambodians."

"Very good!" Carter released his grip on Jason. "By the way, would you mind collecting all the illegal weapons that you and your friends have on you?"

Jason looked angrily at Carter and Chev. He could see that Carter was definitely carrying a piece. But whoever these men were, they sure as shit knew their business. And their business was probably related to shaking people down. "Okay bros, let's fork up the tools of our profession." Amid groans of discontent and disappointment, Jason collected an assortment of lethal weapons and handed them to Carter. "I'm sure you know that we know where to get some more."

Carter gave some of the guns and knives to Chev. "I hope that we meet next under better circumstances."

"Yeah, sure," Jason replied over his shoulder, as he and his friends walked away. "Whatever!"

"Well," Carter said, turning toward Chev, "I would say that was a nice diversionary activity."

"Thanks, Doc!"

"For what?"

"For handling the situation so . . . smoothly and effectively."

"Think nothing of it. Now let us proceed to your habitat."

"Follow me!" Chev responded, leading Carter through a series of alleys and backstreets. When they reached a dilapidated building that looked like all the others, with broken windows and garbage strewn all over, Chev stopped. "This is my place," Chev said proudly.

The only difference between Chev's building and the surrounding ones was the bright red painted words scrawled on the brick: POL POT LIVES! LONG LIVE THE KHMER ROUGE AND THE REVOLUTION!

13

MANHATTAN, NEW YORK

"It's not possible!" Detective Diaz insisted.

"I tell you that it is true! Richard Sao, who claimed that his restaurant was firebombed by me was and still is a member of the Khmer Rouge."

"But, he is so—"

"So respectable and convincing?" Senn interrupted. He led Diaz through the door on the far side of the room that had interested her earlier and whose squeaking hinges could have benefited from a good oiling. The smaller room they entered appeared to serve as a study cum library cum eating area. Two walls were lined with floor-to-ceiling metal shelves holding unruly papers, books, and unbound manuscripts. One contained a strip kitchen, toward which Senn led Diaz. "May I offer you a glass of green tea?" Senn asked, very politely. "Your reaction to Sao was a typical Caucasian response to a soft-spoken, professional-looking Asian."

"No, thank you!"

"Green tea, very good for your health. I believe you Americans love to live longer. This tea has been enjoyed by my ancestors for centuries, and each ancestor has lived to see one hundred years."

"How can I refuse a drink from the fountain of youth?" Diaz relented, responding to the mischievous twinkle in Senn's withered face as he spoke. She realized that even if she had examined him more closely earlier—Senn's thin tapered fingers, the long white hair splaying over his shoulders, his small feet and mincing steps—she would still have been convinced that Cambodian men can often be mistaken for women. "So, in your indirect, respectful way, you are trying to tell me that no matter how a Cambodian may appear, it could be totally deceptive."

"You are very smart, Detective Diaz," Senn responded in his naturally high-pitched voice.

"So that observation about Cambodians may apply to you as well."

"Yes," Senn replied, thinking that the good detective was possibly too smart for her own good. And like most Americans she was not very subtle.

It would be important for him not to fall victim to her clearly provocative posture. He must see to it that she leaves the office as a friend or at least someone who would offer him the benefit of the doubt.

"Then is it possible that Mr. Sao was also correct about you?"

"It is possible," Senn replied, sipping his tea, "but not probable!"

"Would you mind explaining that?"

"There are many reasons, but the simplest one is that I have been incarcerated in one of Pol Pot's reeducation camps. I was considered an educated Cambodian, and, therefore, a significant danger to the regime."

"Why?"

"According to Pol Pot's theory, anyone who had any form of Western education, spoke a foreign language, wore eyeglasses, even possessed a dog, was a direct threat to the creation of what he called 'zero civilization,' a society absent of any foreign, specifically Western, influence."

"Presumably the 'zero civilization' was his form of a communist society."

"Quite correct, Detective." Senn led her over to a photo album that was on top of a wooden desk stacked with books and papers. "Look at these pictures very carefully and you will see precisely what Pol Pot meant by creating a new society where there was no evidence of foreign influence." He opened the frayed leather cover and pointed to the top picture on the first page. "These are Cambodian citizens being rounded up in the center of Phnom Penh by the Khmer Rouge. The Khmer soldiers are the ones dressed in what looks like black pajamas."

"There must be hundreds of people being herded together like cattle."

"Hundreds in this picture," Senn agreed, "but precisely two million Cambodians, not including foreigners, were forcibly taken from their homes, taken to so-called reeducation camps, where they were executed, for the most part, by having their throats slit with the sharp, serrated edge of the palm leaf."

Diaz looked at Senn with incomprehension showing in the wrinkle of her brow. "What's this?" she asked, pointing to the picture on the lower half of the page.

"Those five thousand skulls piled on top of one another is what is euphemistically called the killing field."

"Where are the bodies?"

Senn turned the pages of the album to several pictures of bodies lying askew on the ground. "They simply decapitated most of the bodies, pulled out whatever gold teeth might have been in the skull, and indiscriminately threw all the cadavers into large dirt pits."

"This is incredible! Almost surrealistic!" Diaz was having a hard time absorbing, both intellectually and emotionally, what Senn was telling and showing her. Her temples throbbed. She felt both

nauseous and numb. The denuded, dismembered
limbs and hollow skulls beckoned for some response other than horror. Dignity. Respect. Perhaps,
even a eulogy. But that was not possible. The pictures were simply a grainy black-and-white repre-
sentation of death, bereft of screams of desperation
and fetid smells of festering bodies, which by its
very nature made the atrocity itself that much less
real.

"What you see in those pictures are the evidence
of the first autogenocide of any ethnic group of people. A killing of one's own people. And no one was
free of guilt. No one."

"You, too?"

"Yes!"

"How?"

"As I told you, I had been taken to what was
called a reeducation camp, which was nothing more
than a simplified . . . Auschwitz to the Jews. No gas
chambers. Just starvation, torture, and execution."

"Were you involved in . . ."

"In order to survive the . . . inexplicable condi-
tions of the camp," Senn interrupted, lowering his
voice to sound more sorrowful, "one was forced to
commit all types of atrocities. Acts that one could
never have imagined one was capable of doing."

Diaz waited in silence for Senn to continue.

"Yes, I was forced to do things that I had never
imagined were humanly possible." Senn swallowed
hard, attempting to collect his emotions.

"Maybe we should just stop here," Diaz said,

noticing Senn's watery eyes and increasingly more lugubrious state. "I can come back another day."

"No, that will not be necessary. Please feel free to remain here and finish questioning me. Your questions force me to confront the trauma of that terrible period of time in my country's history."

"I appreciate your cooperation, Mr. Senn, but I think we have reached a point where to continue would be no longer . . ." she halted in order to find the right word. "Productive" sounded too opportunistic and crass. ". . . useful to both sides."

"I admit to you, Detective Diaz, that I was forced to cooperate with the Khmer Rouge against my will. But, as you can imagine, had I refused, I would not be here today to talk to you. Or publish anti-Khmer propaganda."

"Mr. Senn, I understand . . ." Diaz was feeling very uncomfortable with Senn's defensiveness.

"In one sense, Mr. Sao is right. I collaborated with the Khmer Rouge in order to stay alive. But the so-called gentleman who ran that torture camp single-handedly was your innocent-appearing, seemingly respectable, Mr. Richard Sao."

"Are you certain?" Diaz asked, jolted by Senn's words.

"Detective Diaz, do you know the commander of your police precinct?"

"Of course!"

"Well, you don't forget the commandant of a Khmer Rouge camp. Because he is not only your superior by rank, but he is also your torturer. And that imprints him in your memory."

"Are you saying then that Mr. Sao is one of the leaders of the Khmer Rouge here in New York?"

"What I'm saying, Detective, is that he is the leader of the Khmer Rouge in New York, Boston, Anaheim, and several other cities."

"If what you say is correct, then . . ."

". . . then he firebombed his own restaurant."

"Why?"

Senn took a long time answering, and then spoke slowly and firmly. "I think that is now up to you to discover."

With that statement it was clear to both of them that the interview was over.

14

LOWELL, MASSACHUSETTS

Lowell, Massachusetts had seen the best of times and the worst of times. Located twenty-five miles northwest of Boston, the town only began to flourish in the early nineteenth century after an American businessman copied the secrets of a textile manufacturer in Manchester, England and turned his notes and drawings into a factory that he located in Lowell. The city grew into one of America's major textile manufacturing centers for well over a hundred years, until the mid-1960's, when the U.S. economy mercilessly punctured its bloom of success.

Lowell was a city in search of an identity for
several decades until the misfortunes of the Cambodian refugees gave it a second chance for success. These industrious new pilgrims arrived in the
early and mid-1980's with nothing to lose and
transformed what had become a ghost town into a
thriving high-tech area. Alongside the transforma-
tion to a ten percent Cambodian population, however, came the concomitant social dysfunction
typically associated with newly arrived, poor
refugees—teenage vandalism, prostitution, extortion, and a gamut of other crimes that Lowell had
not seen for years.

The center of urban blight in this city of 105,000
people were the busy streets of Pine and Merri-
mack, which sprouted with Cambodian jewelry
stores, Cambodian markets, and Cambodian restaurants. At dinnertime the air was thick with the smell
of spiced meat and pickled whitefish.

The core of criminal metastasis was the Pailin
Plaza, a mini-mall that took its name from the gem-
rich Cambodian region that was the heart of the
Khmer Rouge insurgency. As in many malls around
the United States, teenagers dressed in the latest
jogging outfits and hairdos, smoked outside the
stores, harassed potential customers, and catcalled
to attractive females dressed in colorful sarongs as
they walked past.

"If beauty could kill," Yin Siv shouted to Marie,
a sixteen-year-old Cambodian walking by, "then
death would be a welcome invitation." He mo-

tioned to his friends to turn down the volume on the boom box.

"Little man, play with your boyfriends!" Marie responded, clearly unperturbed by Yin. While she was svelte, it would be clear to anyone who worked out at a gym that Marie was a habitual attendee.

"What did you say?" Yin made believe he hadn't heard the insult. He primped his black leather jacket, reminiscent of the 1950's, and patted his amulets—pewter skulls, chains, skulls and crossbones. His five buddies, all dressed alike, waited to see what Yin would do.

"Turn up your hearing aid," Marie responded brazenly, but tightened her grip on the paper grocery bag she was carrying, filled with ingredients for the evening's meal. She maintained eye contact with Yin, noticing every motion he made, and knew that she was making him nervous. Neither her manner nor her appearance corresponded to the typically meek Cambodian girl he thought he might be encountering.

"You certainly have quite a mouth!" Yin yelled back as if it were a threat. Already insecure at age seventeen about his relatively short stature, he could not let this young girl humiliate him in front of his friends.

"I think the same thing could be said for you!" Marie quickened her pace.

"You seem frightened of me, little girl!" Yin moved alongside her. His buddies followed behind, egging him on by questioning his masculinity and decrying her insolence.

"Why shouldn't I be?" she replied meekly, suddenly shifting her demeanor.

"That's the first smart words you've said!" Yin turned toward his jeering buddies, raising a clenched fist as a sign of success.

"I don't want any trouble." Marie craftily shifted her voice to a higher, more frightened Cambodian pitch. "If you were in my position, I think that you would be scared."

"You have a point!" Yin relaxed his aggressive offensive posture. "Do you know who we are?"

"No!"

"We are Khmer Rouge!"

"What is that?"

"Don't tell us you don't know! We belong to an organization that killed millions of people in Cambodia. We're afraid of nothing. And we're going to take over this town . . . and state. Maybe we're going to be the largest gang in America."

"Why are you so proud that they killed their own people?"

"Because . . ."

"Because why?"

"Because . . . because they killed enemies of true Cambodians. That's why!" Yin was becoming annoyed by the girl's lack of respect. He motioned for his friends to follow more closely as she turned into a dirty alleyway between a grocery store and a gift shop.

"What is the name of your leader?"

"That's a secret!"

"Someone who killed millions of Cambodians is a secret? I find that strange!" She could see that he was becoming increasingly uncomfortable. How fascinating it was, she thought, to observe a bully thrown off balance through the use of nothing more than words and her unusual behavior.

Halfway down the alley she stopped and turned around. Only Yin followed her.

"I'm a direct descendant of that secret leader!" Yin proclaimed proudly, puffing out his chest in a primordial act of pride.

"And you're proud of that?" Marie looked straight into his eyes, daring him to respond.

"Of course, I'm proud! The Khmer Rouge is a brotherhood. All for one and one for all!"

"That saying comes from *The Three Musketeers*, a novel by Alexandre Dumas. Not the Khmer Rouge!"

"How do you know?" Yin asked the question but didn't really want an answer, hoping to find a way to end this little encounter. The girl was sassy. She had become American. That's what the American girls were like. Not like mealymouthed, submissive Cambodian women. He was becoming nervous. Why should this girl try to make him not be proud to say that he was Khmer Rouge? They stood for male dominance and national pride. But, most of all, they were tough. Very tough. And that's what he wanted to be. Tough! Usually all he had to do was mention that he belonged to the Khmer Rouge and everyone from shopkeepers to strangers showed him respect—and never charged him for anything he bought. The Khmer Rouge was like the Italian Mafia used to be. And if he had anything to do with it, he would see that they took the Mafia's place. And he was going to be its leader.

"Because I read!"

"Whatever!"

"Clearly, you don't read!"

"Hey, watch what you say!"

"Or what?"

"You must be kidding me!"

"The only thing that I find funny is you! Look at yourself! Black leather jacket. Black leather boots! You're a parody, if you understand the word *parody*, of an outdated old 50's thug! You're trying so hard to look and act tough that you remind me of a monkey!" She paused, watching him turn red and clenching his fist.

"If you say one more word . . ."

"You'll what?" she said defiantly, balancing the grocery bag between her hands.

"Don't you understand? I'm a member of the Khmer Rouge! We kill people for disrespecting us!"

"I don't believe you."

"Are you calling me a liar?"

"You talk a lot, but say nothing! You are just like the big bad wolf: 'I'll huff and I'll puff till I blow your house down.' But he didn't. And you don't.

You're a blowhard who's never even killed a cock-roach."

"Oh yeah, well I'll show you . . ."

Before Yin could finish his sentence, Marie threw the bag of groceries at his head, throwing him off balance. Then using jujitsu, she flipped him to the ground, jabbed her right elbow into his chest, pinning him down. She grabbed his larynx with her other hand and held it so tightly he could barely breathe.

"The leader of the Khmer Rouge was Pol Pot, a pseudonym for Saloth Sar." She whispered in his ear, "Never utter the name 'Khmer Rouge' unless you are prepared to fight with Cambodian-Americans who are sick of violence and want to be good citizens. Cambodians like you are a disgrace to us and for that you must pay a price."

Yin felt both her hands tighten around his larynx like a vise.

"I could kill you if I wanted to," Marie whispered to Yin as he lost consciousness. "But I'll leave that for another time."

15

CAMBRIDGE, MASSACHUSETTS

"Welcome to Little Cambodia," Chev swept the decaying landscape with his outstretched arms. "Let me show you the legacy Pol Pot, Ta Mok, and Khieu Samphan left us." The cell phone clipped to Chev's belt rang in some strange melodic pattern. "Excuse me for a moment."

Carter surveyed streets filled with yellowed newspaper, dirt, and litter as Chev walked a few feet away and flipped open the mouthpiece of his phone. "You did . . . ? Are you . . . ? Do you have any idea . . . ?" Chev's voice drifted off as he walked further away. Carter heard only snatches of the conversation.

"I'm sorry, Allison," Chev returned, reattaching his cell phone to his belt. "Some very disturbing news."

"Would it be too presumptuous to ask what the disturbing news might be?"

Before answering, Chev led him through a metal gate that he opened up with a rusted key. They walked down some rickety wooden stairs to the basement of a house that turned into a damp, dark tunnel. Carter followed Chev's lead and crouched down to avoid hitting his head against rusted metal pipes and frayed wires. "I received a call from a cousin who lives in Lowell, not too far from here. She informed me that she got into a fight with the leader of a gang that has been going around the city intimidating shopkeepers . . . women . . ."

"Is she OK?" Carter scraped his head against the rough stone sides of the tunnel.

"The other kid got the worst of it."

"What was the problem?"

"My cousin is active in one of the largest Cambodian community centers in Lowell. This other kid, a hoodlum who pretends to be the leader of the Khmer Rouge gang in the city, tried to molest her." Chev paused and laughed out loud. "She almost eliminated him."

The flippancy with which Chev made this announcement bothered Carter, but he decided to let it go unremarked. "Why do you sound so disturbed?

You're telling me that she did what she had to do in order to protect herself." In the distance, Carter saw a light. He hoped this meant that there would soon be a larger space in which to move about. He felt a bit too old to be crawling about in basement tunnels. Like many men in his age group who jogged on a daily basis, he was beginning to develop some osteoarthritis of the spine.

"She also informed me that a Cambodian restaurant in New York was firebombed, and that some old-guard Khmer Rouge party members may have been involved."

"A case of retaliation?" Carter asked.

"I don't think so," Chev replied.

"Then what else could it be?"

"There are many complicated and contradictory reasons that would require time to explain. Perhaps tomorrow. . . . Well, here we are," Chev said, standing upright.

The proverbial light at the end of the tunnel that Carter had crawled toward was, in fact, a large warehouse-type structure where countless Asians stood at long wooden tables busily working at a variety of tasks. Carter was grateful to finally get off his aching knees. "Is your cousin in any danger now?" Carter was content to wait until the next day for the explanation of the firebombing in New York. After all, he and Chev would be working together for quite a while.

"As strange as it might sound," Chev answered, "I'm not really afraid for her. She has been taught to handle herself very well. I'm bothered by the fact that she had to engage in that type of activity."

"What do you mean?" Carter asked.

"All over the United States, in communities where there are Cambodian refugees—Lowell, Boston, New York, Los Angeles, St. Louis, Anaheim, and many smaller communities—organizations have arisen that call themselves Khmer Rouge in order to extort and intimidate—and frequently kill—Cambodian refugees. This disturbs me greatly because it gives Cambodian-Americans a bad name."

"You have to admit," Carter chortled, "the Khmer Rouge is not often associated with mercy, compassion, and charity."

"Believe it or not, Allison, most Cambodian refugees are looking for a sense of community. The Americanized Cambodian communities take care of their own people and provide them with work, shelter, food, and medical care. Look around you at what we are creating. Call it 'self help,' if you will. But we are trying to harness the strength of our people to build a decent life in America, while the Khmer Rouge would like us to, once again, be subservient and pay homage to killers."

The "warehouse" had been divided into several distinct sections by the clever placement of tables and desks. Chev and Carter strolled in and out of the areas in which Cambodians of all ages and both sexes worked on different types of simple machines, computers, and lathes, and with simple materials like straw, ribbon, and paper.

Carter smiled at the Cambodians with whom he could make eye contact. They were not surprised to see a stranger, but no one smiled back. A group of workers were using chemical products, and Carter couldn't help but think that they resembled the basic ingredients for incendiary bombs. This place should be more closely investigated, he thought.

"I'd like you to meet one of the most distinguished members of our community." Chev pointed to a tall, bald-headed Cambodian in his late sixties, dressed in an orange sarong. "Duch, I want you to meet a friend."

"How do you do, Duch?" Carter shook the man's hand.

"Duch is a teacher who was trained in Phnom Penh with the help of U.S. foreign aid. He trained other Cambodians how to speak English. Is that right, Duch?"

"You are very generous in your praise." Duch placed the palms of his hands together and bent his head down in humility. His fingertips touched his forehead in a sign of friendship and respect. "I'm a born Christian who was baptized by your churches . . ."

"Churches?" Carter asked. "Isn't one Christian church good enough?"

"Yes, several churches." Duch continued with great pride, pulling from his overalls pocket several crumpled papers that looked like certificates. "Presbyterian, Baptist, Church of Christ, and two or three more."

"Duch is a very modest man." Chev chuckled at the sight of Carter's incredulity. "He forgot to tell you why your American churches were so interested in converting this saintly appearing gentleman."

"What did you do that made so many churches take an interest in you?" Carter asked.

"I worked with Khmer Rouge soldiers, helping them reeducate enemies of the state."

"Why don't you tell them exactly what you did, Duch?"

"Please, Chev," Duch replied, "I have already done my penance. All the American ministers and priests agreed when they interviewed me that I had done some bad things. But, I also helped the Americans rebuild the temples and the roads leading out of Phnom Penh. That is when I was given these certificates." He handed Carter several faded pieces of paper with company letterhead—AID, International Refugee Aid, Red Cross.

"We commend Duch for his personal leadership and team-building skills," Carter read out loud from one certificate. "That is very impressive."

"Thank you so much, honorable sir." Duch again bowed his head in respect.

"I found Duch running a crushed-ice stall in downtown Phnom Penh and brought him here to the United States so that he could remind us of the past."

"I can't thank Haing Chev enough for the kindness, generosity, and support he has given me." Duch folded his papers and placed them back in his pocket.

Duch bowed his bald head even lower this time, to indicate greater respect.

"Forgiveness is mine sayeth the Lord," Haing Chev proclaimed, quoting sardonically from the Bible.

As Duch raised his head, Chev took a stiletto knife out of his back pocket, snapped it open, and in one fluid motion cut Duch's left carotid artery, crisscrossed his body, and cut between his fourth and fifth vertebrae. Duch fell facedown onto the floor, blood pulsing out of his artery.

"Duch's real name was Kang Khek Ieu," Chev said to Carter with disdain, casually wiping the blade of his knife on a piece of cloth lying on a tabletop nearby. "He was personally responsible for the execution of twenty thousand Cambodians. Four of them were my father, mother, and two brothers."

16

NEW YORK CITY, NEW YORK

In a vast auditorium located in a converted Masonic lodge, the predominantly Indonesian community of Manhattan had created a Buddhist temple that was used by a variety of ethnic groups belonging to the Buddhist faith. Both the interior and exterior of this particular temple, used by residents of three boroughs of New York City, was a creative combination of multicolored plaster reliefs, faded antique tapestries, and an assortment of faux paintings which suggested the Borobudur Temple of Yogyakarta in Indonesia (which, ironically, is a predominantly Muslim country). The New York City reincarnation of this Indonesian temple had less to do with faith than with the fact that a wealthy Indonesian benefactor wanted to bestow part of his good fortune upon the Buddhist community before he and other city officials were carted off to jail for fraudulent activities.

Both Sonn Senn and Richard Sao felt a bit uncomfortable as they walked together through the temple's entrance. It was not Angkor Wat, the most famous Buddhist Temple complex in Cambodia. But years of attendance had minimized their discomfort, and they now appreciated the unique architectural style of their "new" temple, constructed to a scale one fifth the size of the original.

Standing inside the giant stupa, a dome-shaped structure, they glanced at the three hundred stone carvings which depicted the early life of Siddhartha during his passage to enlightenment. As usual, they started at the eastern staircase on the first of five levels and walked clockwise around the gallery following the sequence of Buddha's life.

"I understand you had a visit from a lady detective?" Senn asked in Cambodian.

"Yes!" Sao responded. "Of no consequence. As the Americans call it, 'simply routine.'"

They both walked slowly and spoke softly, looking behind them periodically to make certain that no one was close enough to hear them converse.

Senn pointed to a fifteen-latticed stupa that contained statues depicting Buddha's departure from the material world. "Wouldn't it be wonderful if mortals like you and I could depart this world without disgrace at any time that we might want?"

"I prefer the beautiful pictures of the surrounding mountains with their snowcapped peaks and jagged, rough-hewn terrain." Sao responded in what seemed to be a non sequitur, but knowing that the conversation between them had nothing to do with either the temple or religion.

Senn wanted to know precisely what transpired between Sao and Captain Diaz. Sao wanted to know what happened when Diaz had visited Senn's office. Neither man trusted the other. But trust was a commodity that they could not afford. Life had taught both men that Americans traded trust beneath the concepts of building relationships and team effort. But these concepts were alien to Cambodians. The only belief they held and instilled in their children was: Do unto others those things they would do unto you; but do it first.

"Have you ever seen the real Borobudur Temple, my friend?" Senn asked.

"No, I have never had that opportunity," Sao responded, knowing that Senn was clearly trying to impress him with his extensive experience, wealth, and importance. Perhaps, Sao thought, once upon a time in Cambodia. But not here in the United States. Still, Sao was determined not to be confrontational.

"It is quite exquisite," Senn continued. "It took ten thousand men one hundred years to build that gargantuan temple beneath the penumbra of the formidable volcanoes which the Japanese believed were the houses of God."

"I know I must make some time in my busy schedule to visit this incredible Buddhist wonder," Sao responded, trying to signal Senn that for the moment he accepted his higher status. But if Senn persisted, Sao would not hesitate to leave the meeting which Senn had requested. "It is unfortunate that your brother could not witness the prosperity we have created in this new country."

"Yes, it is a pity."

"Do you miss him?" Sao asked, stopping abruptly.

"I hope that the misfortunes that befell you and your restaurant are not irreparable." Senn completely ignored the question about his brother. Under other circumstances, Sao would have died merely for having asked that question. Sao knew all too well that Senn's brother had been killed during the massacres and that it was he, Senn, who had directly ordered the execution of his brother. He, like thousands of other Cambodians, had been more than happy to kill members of his own family in order to prove his fealty to the cause. But Sao had made his point about being humiliated and Senn thought that perhaps he had pushed him a little too much. Upon reflection he decided that he should have had a lighter touch.

"Damages came to about one hundred thousand dollars. But with good fortune, I think I will be able to restore the business back to where it was before the fire."

"That certainly is very good news"—Senn smiled—"both for you and our beloved Cambodian community."

"As long as no other Cambodian restaurant moves into the neighborhood, then the gods will be looking favorably upon me."

"I certainly doubt that anyone else could think that they would be able to create such fine cuisine as you have."

"Thank you, Sonn Senn," Sao replied. "Those words give me great courage and strength to complete the renovation of the restaurant." Sao was relieved to hear Senn virtually guarantee that no other Cambodian would move into his culinary territory.

"I'm glad that you feel much better. For a moment I was concerned that you were too preoccupied with other matters."

"Now that I have heard the words you have spoken, my mind feels as if it had been cleansed in a bath of chamomile."

"Then you are not only well rested, but you should also smell good."

They both broke out into laughter.

Sao felt comfortable that Senn would be true to his word. He would not allow any other Cambodian to open a restaurant while Sao was rebuilding his own. Senn had that power. If he granted you a business territory, then it was yours as long as you cooperated with him. But at the same time, if you did not follow Senn's dictates, it would be up to you to muster the necessary money, power, and force to counteract the demands of the Khmer Rouge.

Sonn Senn was one of the elders of the Khmer Rouge in the United States. There were many others, but Sao did not know who they were. And he could never be certain that either he or his family members, either in the United States or Cambodia, would ever be safe from men like Senn. Like many other Cambodians who had once been a member of the Khmer Rouge, Sao remained hostage to his past, present, and worse yet, his future.

"Does Captain Diaz know who started the fire?"

"No, I simply let her suspect what we had agreed upon."

"Very good," Senn replied, content that Sao had accepted the temporary destruction of his livelihood, and would be more "supportive" in the future.

"I showed her your article in the newspaper and I told her that I suspected you. I may have mentioned your relationship to the Khmer Rouge. But I did not make a big point about that."

"Excellent!"

"Thank you!"

"Buddha is merciful! Let us leave and drink some green tea together."

17

The City of Angels, a sprawling megalopolis, is far away from Cambodia both geographically and spiritually. On the other hand, there are as many Koreans, Chinese, Japanese, Vietnamese, and Cambodian refugees in the city as there are Mexican immigrants. All one has to do is drive into one of the many rental car agencies clustered around Aviation Boulevard, one traffic light away from the Los Angeles International Airport, to find dozens of Cambodian mom-and-pop businesses.

One of the smaller rental car companies was run by the Mok family, distantly related to the infamous

Ta Mok, who helped Pol Pot execute millions of Cambodians. But unlike their relative, who remained in his native land to stand trial, the Mok family in America, consisting of a middle-aged father, wife, two sons, and a daughter, had arrived in the late seventies to build a new life. Sponsored by a Christian charity association, the family was placed with parishioners who clothed, fed, and even financed them in their first business, "Mok's Car Rental." The Moks were rightfully proud of the fact that they had started with one car and now had a fleet of over two hundred "formerly used" cars. And like all good entrepreneurs, the family had found its market niche, expressed in the logo "We Rent to Anyone!" It was at their establishment that the under-twenty-five-year-old high-risk drivers were given their chance to do damage on the road, with the high premium insurance fees helping to expand Mok's business.

The Mok family were reputed to be responsible businesspeople who were avid members of their church and community. By Cambodian standards they had assimilated and become full-fledged Americans, even going so far as to anglicize their children's names. Taking the letter *M* from their last name, the parents had decided to use it for their children's first names as well—Mark, Matthew, Martha. At school, their friends affectionately referred to them as the "M&M's."

At exactly 4:30 P.M., a Jaguar 2000, S-TYPE 4.0, with its usual assortment of structural and mechanical problems, pulled into Mok's Car Rental. Four young Asian men exited the car carrying an assortment of automatic and semiautomatic weapons. The inscriptions on their black leather jackets were not unlike the ones on the jacket that the thug in Lowell had worn—hollowed skulls, crossbones, and other icons symbolizing death. They ran into the crowded rental office and without saying a word, motioned all the workers toward the back room. The precision with which these men worked showed them to be both professional and targeted. As they forced each person into the room, they were clearly examining faces. Almost half were African-American or Hispanic. Several were Caucasian. All were extremely scared, but they were also curious. No one was hurt. No money was asked for or taken. No one demanded the location of a safe. These men were looking for something, but they weren't saying what it was.

Ten silent minutes later a large burgundy minivan pulled into the car lot and parked right in front of the office. The vanity license plate bore big bold black letters spelling the name MOK. Each of the four men in black leather jackets assumed strategic positions in the office, warning their hostages with hand signals to remain completely silent.

The Mok family spilled out of their van with the expectation of hearing about another profitable day from their employees. The two teenage boys were teasing their sister, who ran in and out of the rental cars accusing her brothers of trying to pull her hair.

Collectively, the entire family could not have been
in better spirits. Each member had a role in the
business they jokingly called their "M&M Empire."
If Hertz and Avis and Budget could do it, one day
they, too, would be successful enough to go public
and make a fortune. Wasn't that the American
dream? But as they walked into their office and saw
four Asian men with weapons pointed straight at
them, each began to think that their future might be
sharply curtailed.

Mr. Mok had been waiting for a long time for
such a visit, although he had never said anything to
his wife or children about its possibility. His face
blanched as he spoke. "What do you want?"

A stocky gang member pointed his gun at Mark,
the eldest son, and motioned him into a red Chevrolet; he ordered Matthew, the younger one, into a
green Volkswagen.

"I'm not getting in!" Matthew broke the silence.

The stocky one fired his Uzi into the air above
Matthew's head.

"Kill me!" Matthew screamed defiantly. "You
want to kill me anyway!"

The stocky man nodded to one of his accom-
plices, who knocked the boy to the ground, bound
his hands and feet, and forced him into the passenger seat of the car. In contrast, Mark, not wanting to
receive the same treatment as his brother, entered
the Chevrolet compliantly. One gang member got
into each car, started their respective engines, and
positioned them so that they were facing each other

on the lot. They raced their motors so that the sound of the roaring engines made their task that much more intimidating.

Mrs. Mok started to cry and held her daughter closely at her side. Mr. Mok was restrained by one of the men so that he was completely helpless. No one had to tell him that he was about to watch his sons die.

The stocky man nodded his head and the chicken race began. The two cars passed each other slowly, picking up speed as they each circled the car lot. By the time they had completed their circle and were approaching each other at a speed upwards of fifty miles per hour, the two drivers opened their front doors and rolled out onto the ground.

The cars met head on.

"A . . . a . . . a . . . a . . . a . . . a . . . h . . . h . . . h . . . h . . . h . . . !" Mrs. Mok screamed as she watched her sons disappear in a ball of fire and smoke.

"I'll kill you for that!" Mr. Mok spit in his captor's face. "You savage!"

"You're right, Mr. Mok! I am a savage! Is that why you had my whole family killed in Cambodia? But wouldn't you agree that you were not nearly as gracious as I? You simply decapitated my brothers before they had a chance to say anything."

"That wasn't me, you fool!" Mr. Mok screamed.

"Mr. Mok, take a look at yourself twenty years ago. I will never forget the glee on your face as you sliced off their heads; heads of innocent Cambodians."

Mok looked at the faded photograph the man shoved before his face. Mok said nothing.

"Spare the mother," the man ordered. "I want the mother to live in the hell of the knowledge that she had witnessed the death of her whole family, standing hopelessly by, unable to do anything but cry. That she alone was spared, to be tormented for the rest of her life."

One of the gang members forcefully separated Martha from her mother and threw her into her father's outstretched arms. The young man then put on thick asbestos gloves, bound the father and daughter with a metal chain and, not waiting for any further orders, poured gallons of hydrochloric acid on both. As their screams rose, Mrs. Mok fainted.

"Chev," the stocky man spoke into his portable telephone, "the Moks are in the heavens, as instructed. Except, of course, for one." He could barely hear the congratulations conveyed from his friend as the screams continued.

18

MANHATTAN, NEW YORK

Driving slowly down the crowded streets of Broadway, Detective Diaz enjoyed the heterogenity that existed in her precinct. A Korean vegetable stand abutted a Spanish bodega that sold beans, rice, and plantains. A Pakistani-run newsstand with daily papers from around the world encroached on a liquor store secretly owned by Mormons. She scanned the blocks perfunctorily to see if anything looked out of place. In a city of ten million people, determining an aberration of any sort was, at best, a miracle. Unless, of course, you had been born and raised like Diaz had, on the streets of New York. She had decided years before that there was no such entity as a "normal" neighborhood. But Broadway, from 108th Street to 42nd Street was a true amalgamation of personalities, cultures, and idiosyncrasies.

With traffic at a standstill she had time to reflect on what Sonn Senn had told her. Richard Sao, the victimized restaurant owner had actually been a killer and an ardent member of the Khmer Rouge. According to Sonn Senn, Sao was a former commander of a Khmer Rouge internment camp and had been instrumental in killing legions of innocent Cambodians. Furthermore, he had destroyed his own restaurant. But Sonn Senn had more or less admitted to being a Khmer Rouge member as well, even if under duress. Who knew what atrocities he was responsible for? Despite his frail countenance, Diaz had a sense that he was dangerous. For him, the truth was a double-edged sword.

The question of guilt still remained. Each man had accused the other of being the culprit behind the restaurant fire and, more importantly, of controlling the activity of Khmer Rouge gangs in several cities. How ironic, she thought, that only ten years ago these Cambodian scum had just been sweet little children who were grateful for the kindness and support of the very people they were now trying to intimidate and extort.

Passing Sao's restaurant, she noticed that the hastily assembled plywood that had covered the shattered windows had been taken down. Officially, the site was a safety and construction hazard, as well as the scene of a possible crime.

She parked her car and radioed the dispatcher at the precinct that she intended to investigate. Out of habit, she unsnapped the leather strap covering her gun and quietly entered the restaurant. The smart thing would have been to ask for police backup. But the smart thing wouldn't give her control over a situation from which she could garner glory.

The light filtering in from the street gave her some perspective on the dining room. She carefully maneuvered around the pieces of charred, contorted wood; its distinct odor competing with the dampness and fungus caused by the soaking the room had received from the firemen's hoses. In front of her were shapeless lumps which once were plastic tables and chairs.

In the distance she could hear indistinguishable voices speaking in a language she did not understand. Walking toward the sounds, the rotting boards beneath her feet suddenly gave way and she found herself hanging, by both hands, on to an intact wooden floor beam. If this was the circus, she would smile in the face of danger, swing her body to and fro, and leap across the hole to the other side of the room to the sound of applause. But that was if she were a trapeze artist and not a cop.

From the little she could see, she figured that there was a ten to twelve foot drop beneath her into the basement of the building. But what sharp protuberance would be waiting for her as she fell

straight down? Her high heels were not the ideal
protection against being pierced by a rusted metal
object.

The sound of voices deeper within the former
restaurant grew silent. Clearly, someone had heard
her. She tried to ignore the strain of her muscles
pulling on her back and neck, otherwise she would
have to admit to herself that she could not hold on
much longer. As she hung over the basement, con-
templating a necessary change of position, a bullet
whizzed by her right ear.

That was all the motivation she needed. Swing-
ing her legs to give her body momentum, the same
way she started to swing herself as a kid in New
York City's playgrounds, she swung across the hole
in the floor and landed in an area on the floor that
seemed stable. The first thing she did was take off
her shoes and use the handle of her gun to knock off
both heels. Two more bullets whizzed by her head.

Voices about one hundred feet away were now
shouting at her, screaming all kinds of obscenities,
in what sounded like pidgin English. That would
teach her, she thought, about not using backup.

She made an end run to the back of what was
once a table, toward the right of the voices. As more
bullets flew by she was able to get a fix on the direction of the blast from the gun barrel. She estimated the shooter was less than fifty feet away. She
held her gun with both hands, arms straight out in
isometric tension, the right hand pulling and left
hand pushing, which offered a steady platform from

which to pull the trigger. She fired three bullets. Someone at the other side of the room screamed.

By the time another blast of gunfire came at her, Diaz was across the room. Yet the closer she approached the shooters, the further they seemed to back away from her. After three more exchanges of gunfire, the room became silent.

As she moved toward what she thought was the direction of the shooters, she tripped over an object which, on closer inspection, turned out to be an Asian man with a bullet through his chest. One down, she thought, maybe two or three still to go.

In the next room, where light was streaming in from some alley windows, Diaz saw the burned remnants of a commercial kitchen. This must have been where the fire started, she thought. At the far end of the room she heard a noise. Diaz stretched out both arms, holding the gun tightly. Out of the corner of her eye she saw movement from a beam in the ceiling.

Shots were exchanged, followed by the scuffling of feet. Then, no one shot back. After several minutes of silence, she relaxed the grip on her gun and slowly looked around the room.

What she saw made her stomach do a somersault and tears swell up in her eyes.

Richard Sao swung from a beam with a rope tied around his neck. The skin over his face had been peeled away. On his chest, enscribed with a knife, was KHMER ROUGE.

19

"Duch and others like him are my major problem," Chev said, ordering the body to be carried out of the room.

"You certainly have a definitive way of dealing with a problem." Carter was both repelled and fascinated by the coldhearted way that Chev worked. No warning of his intentions. A swift execution. And no remorse.

"Atherton is a very clever man," Chev said to Carter as they walked through the warehouse, passing workstations producing straw baskets and hats, T-shirts and banners.

"What do you mean?" Carter asked, impressed by the employment he saw around him.

"I think you know precisely what I mean."

"If you mean that he is extremely good at analysis and strategy, I agree with your statement."

"You are acting coy," Chev responded, helping a small Asian boy tie a bow with a ribbon that was stapled to the brim of a straw hat.

"Coy?" Carter repeated disingenuously.

"You don't impress me as a man who typically plays games with words"—Chev shooed the boy away and looked at Carter—"so why are you doing so now?"

"I don't know what you mean."

"I think that you understand me quite well." Chev continued to stare into Carter's eyes, almost daring him to look away, or do something to indicate that he was lying. But he also knew that Carter was a professional. He wasn't going to reveal anything more than he had to.

"What's your point?" Carter was less concerned with the direction of the conversation than impressed by the fact that Chev had created an organization that seemed to help his community.

"We both know that he wants us to work together to find and kill Pol Pot."

"He asked me to work with you in any capacity that you deemed helpful."

"Does that include killing me when you deem appropriate?"

"He asked."

"And what did you answer?"

"I said 'no.' I'm only getting paid for one target. My assignment is to help you eliminate the Khmer enemy. It's that plain and simple."

"And I'm asking you again, does that mean assassinating me at the proper time?"

"Yes."

"Well, at least you are honest."

"I'm not certain that it's honesty for its own sake or if it is professional pride."

"Now that is the most bizarre comment I've heard yet!" Chev laughed. "I don't know whether to hug you or to kill you right now, right here, for even entertaining the idea."

"Neither," Carter replied, nonplussed. "If I had told you that Atherton had not instructed me to kill you, you wouldn't have believed me anyway." Carter was aware of the ridiculousness of their conversation. What type of man would inform a prospective target that he had been asked to assassinate him at some later date? Was he starting to lose his edge? The job on Martha's Vineyard, while accomplished, was not up to Carter's own standards. The fact that he had not answered Chev's question truthfully, but had been believed by him, was not some great psychological coup.

"The mere fact that I asked you the question meant that I had already harbored that suspicion," said Chev. "Now it's my turn to be impressed with your honesty."

"Actually, I told Atherton that I could never kill

someone I worked with and admired." Carter lied. "By the time the month is over, I might even join your cause." He lied again. "Let Atherton do his own dirty work next time."

"I think that I would work with you to find Pol Pot and eliminate some Khmer leaders even if it means always checking my back, just to make sure that you weren't confusing me with a buck in hunting season. But then, again," Chev winked at Carter, "you never can tell what Atherton asked me to do to you."

"Then I'm the dispensable one, and you're the indispensible one, if I understand you correctly."

"You could say that," Haing Chev responded with bravado.

"But what would happen if we dispensed with you?" Carter asked in a provoking tone of voice.

"If that's what you want to try, I'm game." Haing Chev's voice cracked. He was suddenly feeling very uncomfortable. Was his own pride getting in the way of working with Carter? If this was part of Carter's PSYOPS ability, it certainly was working.

"What if I placed both my hands around your neck"—Carter put his hands around Haing Chev's neck as he spoke—"and I squeezed both of your carotid arteries simultaneously? By doing this I could literally cut off the circulation to your circle of Willis, the central core that supplies the blood to your brain."

"You could kill me. Is that what you're telling me?" Haing Chev remained immobile. But he couldn't appear concerned. He would lose face. His credibility in his community would be in question.

"That's correct!"

"Is that what you are going to do right now? In front of everyone?"

"We really won't know until I do it, now will we?"

"You are merely testing me!"

"You can put it that way."

"Continue," Haing Chev responded in a loud, firm voice, "I'm not afraid!"

"Just tell me the point at which you no longer trust me. Raise your right hand and I will stop the pressure. The less pain you want, the less trust you have. I will calibrate our future working relationship accordingly."

"According to your rules, if I let you kill me, that means that I trust you completely. But I will be dead."

"Point well taken! But this is only a test." Carter slowly squeezed Haing Chev's neck.

"I'm starting to have . . . a hard time . . . breathing." Haing Chev wondered how the past few interesting hours had turned into this ugly scene. He was sorry that Atherton had not accompanied them to this warehouse. Carter was a loose cannon. Maybe he should have continued with the shrink in Brookline.

"Soon you will feel light-headed." Carter tightened his strong fingers around Haing Chev's throat, hoping that by squeezing the primary blood vessels to the brain he wouldn't dislodge a cholesterol plaque from one of the arteries and induce a cerebral thrombosis. A paralyzed Haing Chev wasn't the purpose of this game.

"I'm having . . . a hard time . . . seeing clearly."

"That simply means that I'm applying more pressure. Remember, if you want me to stop just raise your right hand."

"No!"

"The next level of pressure will make you feel very light-headed, dizzy. You might even suddenly feel sleepy."

"No!" Haing Chev could barely utter the word.

"In a few seconds you will black out! There is a slight chance that you might be permanently injured." Carter was hoping that this statement would force Haing Chev to consider surrendering.

"No!" Haing Chev uttered the word again as his head slumped down his chest.

"One more degree of pressure. The last one. Do you hear me?"

Haing Chev did not respond. His body simply went limp and incontinent.

20

BOSTON, MASSACHUSETTS

"Call nine-one-one," Carter yelled into the crowd surrounding Haing Chev's body, hoping that someone understood English. "Ask for an ambulance." He did a quick medical exam of the limp body as it lay on the cement floor. Vital signs: thready, almost nonexistent radial artery pulse; no evidence of blood pressure. Neurological signs: fixed dilated bilateral pupils, hypotonia in the extremity muscles. Breathing: barely audible; erratic; unresponsive to external stimuli. Conclusion: Haing Chev was in a coma. The key question was whether the coma was irreversible, but there was no time to wait for an answer. There was only one option available—cardiac resuscitation.

"You!" Carter pointed to a young man standing close to the body. "Breathe into his mouth once after I pound on his chest twice."

Carter pried open Haing Chev's mouth and the young man placed his mouth over it. The scene looked like two guppies kissing. He waited and watched as Carter pounded on Haing Chev's sternum with his hands clasped together. There was something both frightening and exciting about being part of an effort to save his employer's life.

"You're doing fine. . . ."

"Sichan is my name," the man responded, and then took the initiative of waving away the workers who were collecting around the body. "Give us some room. Haing Chev needs to breathe in some air."

"Sichan," Carter said, "pay attention to your patient. And don't give up." As soon as the words left his mouth he realized that he was trying to reassure himself more than he was Sichan. "Breathe in and out deeply. You are acting like an air bag which is trying to inflate his lungs." Carter kept pressing down on the sternum, but there was no indication that Haing Chev was responding to his efforts. Carter checked his watch. About two minutes had passed since they had started CPR. If . . . no, when . . . they were successful in resuscitating Haing Chev there would be no assurance that he would not have some brain damage from the lack of oxygen reaching his brain cells. Three or four minutes would be pushing it.

"Finally," Carter sighed as he saw two paramedics dressed in their standard blue uniforms and colorful EMS patches approach. Their medical bags contained everything from needles, to defibrillators, to a varied assortment of drugs that could assist them in resuscitating a comatose patient.

"What happened?" asked one of the paramedics as he placed an ambubag over Haing Chev's mouth and squeezed it to force air into his lungs. Haing Chev's chest expanded.

"Clear the area!" The other paramedic ripped open Haing Chev's shirt and placed two defibrillator paddles on his chest. One press of a button jolted the body with a massive amount of electricity.

"I've got no breathing yet," the first paramedic shouted to his partner.

"Zip on pulse! I'm going to zap him again!" The paramedic looked around before he shouted "Clear the way" and sent another bolt of electricity through Haing Chev. "Nothing yet." To hell with it, he thought to himself. This guy's a goner if I don't jam some chemicals into him. Without wasting a moment, he took a syringe with a three-inch needle attached and measured the spaces between Haing Chev's ribs to decide where he should insert it. He filled it with epinephrine and pushed the needle straight into Haing Chev's heart. "Come on, mother . . . ! Let's get those muscles jumping."

Carter slipped out of the warehouse unnoticed while everyone watched the drama unfold. He hailed a taxi and instructed the driver to go to Logan Airport. His one instinct was to return home, back to Washington, D.C. Only there could he allow himself to feel something other than the numbness he was experiencing. The taxi driver tried to engage him in trivial conversation, but Carter made it clear that he wanted to be left alone. Alone with his thoughts. Alone with the all too familiar sense of death. What was he going to tell Atherton? That he had accidentally killed his co-conspirator in some foolish act of measuring trust? There was nothing he could say to Atherton, or to himself, that would justify what he had done. Whether by accident or intention, Haing Chev was most likely on his way to the city morgue. No one had to remind Carter that there was no room in his line of business for mistakes. How could he have imagined that he might not jeapordize Haing Chev's life when he played his little game? It's not that he hadn't played the game innumerable times before. But no one had ever died.

What if it wasn't an accident! Perhaps at some level of his unconscious he had wanted Haing Chev dead. Now, or later, the dirty deed would have been done. But Atherton had been quite specific—only after Haing Chev had helped Carter infiltrate the Khmer Rouge gangs and find Pol Pot.

When they arrived at the airport, Carter paid the driver and bought a one-way economy ticket to

Washington, D.C. Was it really only hours ago that Haing Chev had been the taxi driver?

WASHINGTON, D.C.

"I'm quitting," Carter said matter-of-factly to Atherton as they sat at a small table in an empty Bamboo Juice, a health drink franchise on Wisconsin Avenue, where a liquor store had once been located.

"Look at you." Atherton avoided Carter's remark. "You look terrible." He was nursing a green drink, sucking on his straw. As usual, he was dressed in a meticulous blue blazer with his monogram stitched on his breast pocket. A handkerchief splayed out of the pocket like a white gardenia in a blue vase.

"I feel terrible." Carter took another sip of his Diet Coke. "I almost don't accomplish one assignment. Then I accidentally kill a colleague. If it wasn't so awful it would be laughable." He looked at Atherton for support. "I'm tired of killing people."

"It sounds to me that you are tired of killing the wrong people." Atherton took the liberty to clarify Carter's intent. "Can you believe that this godforsaken concoction contains enough grass to make a three-thousand-pound thoroughbred win the triple crown?" He looked at Carter's face and realized that Carter was not sitting with him because he was interested in the drinks served. Atherton knew that he had better measure up to the moment or he would lose a good employee. "Sounds to me that you are bleating a bit with a tinge of self-pity and a heavy dose of guilt."

"Do you hear what I'm telling you?" Carter screamed at Atherton. The entire scene was completely surrealistic, he realized. Here he was, completely disheveled, checkered with bloodstains, only hours after killing Chev. When Carter's plane landed, his only telephone call was to Atherton, requesting an immediate meeting.

"You know that there are enough antioxidants in this drink that I could conceivably live to the age of one hundred, disease-free?" Atherton tried to lighten the atmosphere.

"Atherton," Carter clenched his jaw as he spoke, "this is an assignment I can't take and I don't want."

"I need you. It's too late to find someone else. I'll get you another Cambodian to work with. These . . . things . . . sometimes happen." Atherton almost bit his tongue when he said the last sentence. He wondered if Carter would think he was sincere.

"I'll return the initial deposit with interest," Carter said, ignoring Atherton's remarks. "And to show my good faith, I'll even go see a shrink and get some help so that in a couple of years I might be able to be used again."

"You had a chance with Dr. Hoffman and you made a total sham of it. Do you have any idea how much paperwork I had to fill out for that one visit to the psychiatrist?"

"How can you compare . . ." Carter raised his voice again.

"Have you no pity?" Atherton whispered back, shaking his head with disbelief. "Do you know how hard it is to find someone to insure you for your mental health? Warts and hemorrhoids are all reimbursable, but not anxiety and neurosis."

"I think there is very little else for me to say." Carter stood up to leave.

"Sit down!"

Carter kept standing, looking at Atherton's stern eyes. He realized that the general was genuinely angry. If he left at this particular moment, there would be incalculable consequences. That's all I need, he thought, one more enemy. The last thing he wanted was a final confrontation with Atherton in a juice bar. The situation definitely was ridiculous.

"Forget your pride, sit down!" Atherton reiterated. "I hear what you are trying to tell me."

"Trying?" Carter laughed. "How much more explicit can I get?"

"When I first recruited you, I asked you what was, in your opinion, the least favorable part of your personality." He paused. "Do you remember?"

"Of course, I remember."

"So try not to be so petulant," Atherton interjected solemnly. "If truth be known, I'm not certain that anything that you have told me happened over the last few hours."

"Will you allow me to resign?"

"I'm not sure. It's just that you are presently in no condition to confirm anything, or deny anything, or make a decision like quitting!"

"Then it's time for me to get some extended leave."

"Right now it's time for you to sit down and listen. That's all."

"I've heard what you had to say to me."

"I asked you a question. Do you remember what it was?"

"Something about . . ." Carter started to laugh. His mind couldn't focus on anything but a blade of grass that was stuck to Atherton's front tooth.

"May I ask what is so funny?"

"You have green stuff on your teeth. Makes you look pretty silly."

"Silly?" Atherton rolled his tongue over his teeth.

"No, not silly." Carter was trying to find the right word. "Strange."

"Strange?"

"You know what I mean. Dammit, I don't know what the right goddamn word should be." Carter knew that *silly* and *strange* were words to which Atherton was particularly sensitive. They were adjectives that Atherton expected Carter to keep to himself. According to Atherton, one adjective led to another adjective and then to a verb and then to a noun, and before long a sentence, and finally a paragraph of important knowledge is revealed, completely inadvertently.

"Answer my question!"

"Which one?"

"The one I asked you about yourself!"

"What did I think was the weakest part of my character?" Carter looked at Atherton like a man who had just woken up from a stupor. "Am I right?"

"So far so good," Atherton replied, his tone of voice reassuring.

"I think I said that impatience was the weakest part of my character."

"That one, compulsive fornication, of which you said you were cured, and loving rock and roll, were your three greatest deficits."

"Rock and roll? No way!" He smiled. "You sly fox, you added that one to test my memory."

"Thank God, at least you have some Betz cells left in your gray matter."

"I said that I want to quit. I'm tired. Washed out. Burnt. *Kaput*."

"Got any other words to describe yourself?"

"Exhausted. Sloppy. Inefficient. Unprofessional. Disloyal."

"Disloyal? To whom?"

"To my principles of upholding the Hippocratic oath."

"No, my friend, you mean your 'Hypocritical oath.' "

"Very funny."

"Any more words you can think of which make you feel inadequate and vulnerable?"

"Wow, I didn't have to go to Dr. Hoffman. I should have just come here and let you analyze me in this juice bar."

"Allison," Atherton said, leaning toward Carter, "everything that you said about yourself may be true."

"May be true? That's pretty presumptuous of you to think that you know my faults better than I do. I'm an expert on fault recognition. God only knows that I've practiced it long enough."

"You messed up. So what?" Atherton waited. "It's part of the business. That's why there isn't a line around the block waiting to take your assignments. Why do you think that I gave you this case, even after you didn't give a virtuoso performance in Martha's Vineyard?"

"I really don't know why!" Carter paused. "To give me another chance?"

"I know that beneath that self-pitying, Atherton-loathing self of yours there is a *soupçon* of admiration for me. But, I assure you that neither Christian charity nor forgiveness is one of my major virtues." Atherton paused. "However, although I'll hate myself for admitting it, you are probably right. You probably need some relaxation. A break from . . . work, for a short while."

"Can it be that you actually have been hearing what I've been saying?"

"I'll see if I can come up with someone else for

the assignment. Give me a week," Atherton said, "then I'll know if I can let you off the hook."

Carter smiled. "Now you're talking!"

"So what will you do with a week?" Atherton asked out of what seemed nothing more than idle curiosity. "Go to St. Thomas?"

"No," Carter answered, "the Bronx."

21

Detective Diaz burst into the *Cambodian News* office, her gun aimed straight at the seated figure of Sonn Senn hunched over his desk in the same way she had seen him the last time. "You're under arrest."

"You certainly aren't accusing me of the death of Mr. Richard Sao," Senn responded with his usual soft-spoken demeanor.

"I certainly am!"

"That's quite unfortunate." Senn stood up and shuffled slowly toward her.

"You have the right to remain silent." Diaz

inched backward as Senn approached her. Another foot and she would hit the wall. "Anything that you say will be held against you. You have the right to an attorney. If you cannot afford one, a public defender will be appointed for you."

"Thank you for doing your duty, but let us dismiss all this legal nonsense. It really means so little. Let us not waste both of our times."

"How did you know about Mr. Sao's death?"

"The sounds of the jungle travel as quickly in the noisy streets of Manhattan as they do in my hometown in Battambang Province."

"I would like you to turn around so that I do not have to use unnecessary force in order to handcuff you."

"Of course. I will be happy to oblige you in any way that will make your work easier."

"Why did you kill him?" Before Senn answered she watched his normally warm, inviting eyes turn icy cold. She suddenly knew that she had crossed an important boundary. Perhaps she shouldn't have been so cavalier when she declined her precinct captain's offer of police backup. Something told her that she might have been wrong. Ostensibly, nothing had changed. He was still a frail, ailing old gentleman. But something was different. She could feel it. It was almost as if he knew what she was thinking and what she would say, before she did. Or was she only spooking herself, having found what the coroner had attested to was Sao's body, hanging skinned to his bones. Looking into Senn's eyes,

Diaz had no trouble believing that Senn could have ordered the death and mutilation.

"How can you accuse me of killing him when you don't have any evidence?" Senn asked, as he slowly turned around to allow Diaz to handcuff his hands together behind his back.

"You were the last one to see him alive," she answered, knowing that she was bluffing, "and you had a strong motive."

"And what might that be?" He smiled, sensing that the detective had no significant evidence with which to work.

"He accused you of burning down his restaurant," Diaz offered, "and was going to expose you as a leader of the Khmer Rouge in New York." She walked around him so that she could face him. The handcuffs could wait.

Senn recognized her legal uncertainty. All she had was a dead body. Motives were easy to manufacture. "I'm certain that you were meticulous enough to find out that Mr. Sao maintained a significant amount of insurance on himself, his family, and his business." He paused to assess her reaction. It was as he thought; she hadn't checked on Sao's insurance policies. "As for my being the leader of a detested group of killers, I ask you to notice that I am an old man. I can barely control the functions of my body, let alone a group of undisciplined youths."

"Pol Pot was frail, and he still led a formidable

army of followers." Diaz searched for a response that didn't sound naïve.

"Yes, but even he could not avoid the ultimate thief—death. It stole his body, spirit, and his Khmer Rouge following."

"Did you know him?" Something made her ask that question. It was the familiarity with which he referred to Pol Pot, as someone who understood him.

"In a way." Senn walked back to his desk and sat back down on the chair Diaz had found him in. The office was dimly lit and empty of any employees. "One could say that anyone who survived Pol Pot's genocide knew him in one way or another."

Diaz reholstered her gun and clipped her handcuffs back on her belt. Senn was right. She had no real evidence. Nothing that would stand up in court. Her captain had warned her against being too hasty, lest she destroy a case before it was developed. And he was right.

"While you have no fingerprints with which to connect me with Sao's untimely death, Pol Pot's fingerprints, you could say, were all over the massacre of two million people. Some of my countrymen say that that was an act of a fanatic. Others will tell you that Pol Pot was a hero, a man who dedicated his life to maintaining a pure Cambodian society, eradicating any trace of Western civilization from his country. Pol Pot was following the teachings of his Chinese mentor, Mao Tsetung, who believed in reeducation of the intelligentsia, and eliminating all subversives within the rank and file. Mao had initiated a period of chaos in 1956 which was called the Cultural Revolution. Millions of Chinese died because they weren't radical enough for their leader. This was the primary model for Pol Pot."

"I'm having trouble figuring out if you like him." Diaz realized she had guessed right. Senn had an all-too-familiar knowledge of Pol Pot. Unlike most journalists and American politicos who dismissed Pol Pot in the newspapers as crazy, Senn was describing him with nostalgia, as a true believer who had encouraged atrocious acts to be committed in the name of national pride. Diaz couldn't help but wonder how close Senn was to Pol Pot. And if Pol Pot were alive, would he be looking back on his handiwork as a grand mistake in theory or only a failure in its execution.

"He's beyond liking or not liking," Senn responded with an anger he had not shown before. "*Hate* is not even a strong enough word when so many in your family die because of someone's idiotic beliefs. *Detest* begins to approximate the emotion more fully. But only when one looks at the thousands of bleached skulls piled one on top of the other in the killing fields can you get a real hint of the evil that this man sent into my country. In Judeo-Christian terms, he is what one would call the devil incarnate, an anti-Christ." He paused to collect his emotions. "At least, that is what those who are his enemies say."

"Then why do you support him and his followers in your newspaper?" Diaz no longer feared the aged man sitting before her. Whoever he was, he spoke like a man who was lost; a man who was trying to come to terms with a life that was almost over. But Senn was still very clever. She had no doubt that she was being manipulated. But for what end?

"I only appear to support Pol Pot's cause. I, too, would like to ferret his followers out of their rat holes all over the United States."

"And then what?"

"That answer would be self-incriminating," Senn responded with a wry smile. "Theoretically, I would collect evidence of a legal nature and hand it over to the police," Senn replied disingenuously.

"The same way you did with Sao?"

"That was handled by the same people who will accompany you from my office."

A sudden noise behind Diaz caused her to quickly turn around. There stood three large Asian men in black leather jackets. Each man had a gun pointed at her. They had entered the room without making a sound on the creaking wooden floor. Clearly, they had been trained in the art of assassination.

The quiet of the room was broken only by the sound of a body falling. Diaz had made the unfortunate mistake of becoming hypnotized by a great storyteller.

Silencers on guns were a wonderful invention, Senn thought.

22

WASHINGTON, D.C.

Like most people who try to endure the *Sturm und Drang* of everyday life, replete with passive-aggressive behaviors and limitless frustrations, Carter's apartment was the sanctuary where he re-constituted his mental and physical well-being. Located on the third floor of a seven-story building two blocks from Dupont Circle, Washington, D.C.'s equivalent of Greenwich Village, Carter's apartment was an exercise in dishevelment. His dark one-bedroom apartment was filled with wooden bookshelves sagging under the weight of books, from *Gray's Anatomy* and *The Merck Manual* on medicine, to histories of rock and roll, to handbooks on international terrorism and counterterrorism. A stereo lay hidden beneath piles of cassettes and long-playing records. What wall space remained in the living room was filled with one poster announcing the performance of Little Richard, Chuck Berry, and Jerry Lee Lewis, and another of David Bowie with outstretched arms beneath incandescent lights. On the floor lay an expensive Isfahan rug Carter had acquired in a clandestine operation in Quom, Iran.

The decor reflected his own internal contradictions: the intellectual who was intrigued by a range of topics from an analysis of Stalin's mind to the self-conscious pronouncements of the Velvet Underground during the early 1960's. He treasured a rare first edition book by Iggy Pop and the Stooges in which Iggy tried to explain what he was trying to accomplish with what appeared to be cacophony. Carter was most proud, however, of his collection of autographed, dated historic documents written by important physician/writers. Somerset Maugham. Sir Arthur Conan Doyle. Oliver Wendell Holmes Sr. Anton Chekhov. William Carlos Williams. A. J. Cronin. Walker Percy. Ché Guevara. Even as a child he had been fascinated by physicians who had practiced medicine but yet found the time and had the talent to be writers as well. Carter felt a certain kinship with them, each having sought immortality in his own way, defining his own social reality. Doyle, a practicing surgeon, created the fictitious detective Sherlock Holmes. Chekhov wrote insightful plays and short stories about the Russian character while he ran a tuberculosis ward. Cronin wrote a book that devastated the British medical establishment of the 1930's by revealing its concern for mercantile interests rather than for providing care for coal miners. Williams became a famous poet while he maintained a full-time pediatric practice. Both Percy and Ché never practiced medicine, but Ché became a formidable revolutionary icon the world over because of an idealized charismatic presence. Carter always smiled to himself when he looked at Che's picture, thinking that at least one of them had an ideology for which he was willing to risk his life.

Clearly, Carter identified with them. Not with their writing careers, per se, but their presence in his apartment made him feel that he was not alone in choosing a dual career. Certainly, treating sick patients was sufficient unto itself and the practice of medicine was a well-respected profession. But to Carter, so should be the "profession" of contract assassin.

He had always felt that his second career was as important for society as was his first: eliminate the bad guy at market price. No great overlaying moral imperative; just get rid of murderers who had committed major atrocities without incurring any cost for their misdeeds.

Damn it, he thought, what he needed most of all right now was rest. Not ruminations. Not doubts.

What happened in Boston was water under the
bridge. There was nothing he could do about it now.
He walked over to his stereo and put in his favorite
tape, Buddy Holly's *That'll Be the Day*. The music
was an adolescent lament for love and love lost. As
he pondered the words of the song he poured himself a glass of his favorite vodka, Absolut, and sank
into the well-worn pillows of his couch.

He was alone. But he had memories. The faces
of assorted women with whom he had a significant
relationship raced through his mind in a wild kalei-
doscope of locations—Paris, Madrid, Lisbon,
Moscow, Tblisi, Beijing. Each city was reminiscent
of what Proust had described in his novel *Remem-
brance of Things Past*, a place where the smells,
sounds, textures, and their concomitant emotional
associations gave him a context from which he
could draw some sustenance and mental tranquility.
In Carter's everyday world, filled with high adrenaline, paranoia, isolation, loneliness, and extreme
vulnerability, he had to rely on emotional imprints
that lay in some distant shore of human transaction.
And as the years went by, and he became more
emotionally distanced, he found that he had to work
hard to dredge up some vestige of a memory; be it
a moment of anger, love, indifference, a slight, or
more likely, a threat.

His two serious relationships had resulted in a
barren experience in every conceivable way. There
were no children. His former wife had not wanted
to live the life of an emotional widow, waiting until

Carter would return from each assignment. She had
been a nurse when they met but had decided, while
they were still married, that she wanted to become
a hospital administrator. Carter knew that going
back to school for an advanced degree was really in
retaliation for his frequent absences; she had decided to busy herself so that she would not have to
depend on his presence for meaning in her life. For
several months they lived parallel lives and did not
have to interact. It was only when he confronted her
with what was happening did they agree to separate,
amicably.

After two glasses of Absolut his second intense
relationship seemed an angstrom more interactive
than his first. This time he decided to live with
someone who was creative, someone in the arts,
someone who could broaden his emotional and intellectual scope. He met this woman, ironically, on
Martha's Vineyard. She was exhibiting her water-
color drawings in a tiny gallery on Circuit Avenue,
in the town of Oak Bluffs. Unlike his first wife, she
was petite, svelte, and had smiling brown eyes. Initially, there was endless sex—erotic, forbidden, sur-
reptitious. They also both enjoyed the very simple
pleasures of life like going to a matinee movie, bi-
cycle riding, jumping into the high tide, and pic-
nicking on South Beach.

But, like most relationships based on hedonism
and immediate gratification, leading to the delusion
of love, their live-together-for-a-test lasted about
the same number of years as his first marriage,

short one month, and the reasons for its demise were not all that different. Eventually, this second woman got tired of waiting for him, and painting was not a sufficient sublimation for her emotional needs. Their relationship was terminated, as before, amicably. The unfortunate part was that even after two failed relationships Carter had learned very little about his own dynamics and why he continuously entered relationships that had very little chance of surviving.

He laughed to himself as he lay down on the frayed couch. "Atherton," he shouted out, "you are my wife, except this time our separation may not be so amicable." For a moment, he felt joyful that he was determined to leave the services of VAS. But he had a premonition that this last marriage wouldn't be so easy to end. Atherton was not the type of mate who would let him go without repercussions of some kind.

Atherton could interfere with Carter's job in the State Department's medical unit. But that might expose Atherton to the scrutiny of the DSA (Diplomatic Security Agency), which could not abide by anything that was related to covert operations. Or Atherton could make Carter's personal life difficult—having shills create problems for him, mess up his credit ratings, who knows the range of problems. But the biggest potential consequence, of course, was termination, not only of his services, but of him.

How bad could death be? Carter certainly had

confronted it enough times to be immunized to the notion of death. It was one of those words that created no more than a numbing sensation in his mind.

The word *violence*, however, created quite a lot of anxiety in him. It was loaded with contradictions, ambiguities, and interminable uncertainty. Whichever part of the world he turned to, Carter saw violence. The Balkans, Africa, Indonesia, Pakistan, Afghanistan, Cambodia, Latin America. Worst of all, the United States. Even children were infected with the virus of violence—Columbine, in Colorado; the National Zoo in Washington, D.C. Yet in the truest sense, violence was an equal opportunity phenomenon, devoid of gender, sex, age, or religion. It had become the ethos of the twenty-first century. The more it spread, the deeper it burrowed into the psyche of each individual. Pol Pot and his minion of murderers were only quintessential examples.

Pol Pot, a mild-mannered French schoolteacher, was sent to Paris in the early 1950's to obtain a general education. What would he have learned at that time to help craft a murderer, Carter wondered. Certainly, he would have been exposed to the teachings of the French Communist Party, which, at that time, was one of the major apologists for Stalin, the brutal dictator who had murdered twenty to thirty million Russian/Ukrainian kulaks, and two million of his own military officers. The analogy was ripe to be made. Stalin wanted to transform an agrarian society into an industrial society without any counterrevolutionists. The lesson that Pol Pot and his cohorts learned was to destroy everything that did not fit into your model of a new civilization. Be decisive, ruthless, and merciless. Above all, start your human carnage with those who brought you to power, your early supporters.

And then there were the teachings of Georges Sorel, a brilliant philosopher who in the early twentieth century wrote *Reflections on Violence*, a treatise that was the inspiration for a spate of domestic and international terrorist acts in the 1960's. According to Sorel, the modern intelligentsia, of which Pol Pot was a member, felt alienated from society. This group did not feel constrained by society's moral imperatives or norms. They were isolated from civil society and drew a sharp boundary around themselves, redefining the moral dictates to which they would adhere.

For Pol Pot and his followers, Carter concluded, aggressive affirmation of the group's integrity was as essential as solidarity against an outside group. Heroism became a high virtue. Attempts to reconcile differences between groups by compromise and negotiation were decried. By committing an aggression, the dignity of the individual and the group was elevated and endowed with pride and glory.

"Atherton, you son of a bitch!" Carter shouted in a loud mocking voice. "You knew that eventually I would realize that I and Pol Pot were one."

23

Tom Reed, Undersecretary of State for Political Affairs, wiggled restlessly in his oversized leather chair as the meticulously dressed young man in front of him finished the briefing. The morning intelligence briefing by an INR (Intelligence and Research Bureau) representative was perfunctory, Reed thought, but did it have to be so boring? He wished he could dismiss the junior FSO and tell him that in his entire paper-filled briefcase there was very little that was informative.

"In Southeast Asia," the officer continued,

"Khmer Rouge renegades attacked one hundred fifty-six tourists on a trip to Angkor Wat."

"Anyone killed?"

"No, sir! Some of them were treated for heat exhaustion and psychological stress."

"Did Prime Minister Malavy make any public comment?"

"He held a press conference and announced that the 'bandits' would soon be apprehended and punished for their 'criminal activities.'"

"Were the so-called bandits identified as Khmer Rouge?" Reed strained to hear the answer because the junior officer spoke softly.

"Not officially," the officer responded hesitantly, "but no Cambodian was fooled. They knew that the 'bandits' were the KR. No one is convinced that they have been defeated by the present government. Some even believe that Pol Pot is still alive."

"What?" Reed asked disingenuously. He knew the situation in Cambodia better than anyone else, including his own desk officer.

"Well sir, you know how emotionally volatile the Cambodians are. They believe that Pol Pot is still operating out of Battambang Province. Some put him in the United States."

"The United States?" Reed asked. "How did that rumor get started?"

"I can't tell you how, but rumor has it that Pol Pot is alive and well and in the States, just waiting for a triumphant return to Cambodia. The Cambodian press believe that Pol Pot's death photographs were doctored in order to convince everyone that he killed himself rather than be arrested."

Reed leaned forward, looking into the tired, deep-set eyes of the articulate officer, whose day's highlight would be the briefing he was giving him. What a miserable system, Reed thought. Take bright college graduates into the INR, a moribund three-hundred person bureau that reduplicates information received from the *New York Times* or the *Washington Post*, ask them to ruminate over the important events, and then, if they are lucky, ask them to brief one of the more prominent underlings in the State Department. What a waste of talent, time, and money. As far as Reed was concerned, the INR could be totally dismantled without losing an iota of intelligence that was valuable to formulating foreign policy. Let the CIA, DOD, and NSA collect and analyze intel. State should determine whether it was meaningful or not.

Reed recalled that he had once picked up a copy of the *New York Times* and thrust it in front of this briefer and asked this young FSO the difference between what he was telling Reed and what the *Times* had printed on its front page. The young officer was speechless while Reed reprimanded him for manufacturing intelligence that was worth only the price of newsprint. The intel officer, new at his job, went back to the bureau and broke down crying. Reed had been told that the officer was consoled only by the fact that his boss was aware of Reed's idiosyncratic behavior and that the interchange with Reed didn't diminish the young officer's performance in his boss's eyes. From that time forward the officer made certain that he was well-briefed before he saw Reed, but his manner was still hesitant.

"Our sources say that the rumor started in Malavy's office," the intel officer responded, uncertain whether he should be presumptuous enough to imply that the prime minister, himself, may have been the primary source.

"Goddamn, son of a bitch!" Reed muttered to himself.

"I'm sorry, sir," the intel officer interjected. "Was I out of line in any way?"

"Not at all," Reed replied, hoping that the intel officer would accept his excuse. "I just had a tangential thought. It had nothing to do with what you were saying." He was inwardly furious that Malavy might even be considered the source of any rumor concerning Pol Pot. Discretion is what he and Malavy had agreed upon. The world would learn that Pol Pot was not dead at the right time! Of course, he thought cynically, most Americans wouldn't even know who Pol Pot was. They might remember that some movie had been made about a madman who killed millions of his own people. But ask any American where Cambodia was located and you'd get a dumb stare as an answer.

"What do you suggest we do to counteract those false rumors?" Reed wondered why he was asking a junior officer what the next course of action might be. He sounded desperate, which was the last impression he wanted to convey to this young FSO.

"Without knowing too much about the specific situation," the officer responded, pleased with a chance to recoup his self-esteem and to demonstrate his analytical skills, "I would say that the best thing to counter this type of rumor is to create a counter rumor that calls into question the credibility of the source."

"You mean something along the lines of a rumor that might imply that Malavy was not competent to be the prime minister of Cambodia?"

"That's it, sir," the intel officer responded with the enthusiasm of a novitiate who had just been indoctrinated into the sacrosanct halls of covert operations. "An effective PSYOPS campaign would discredit the prime minister and, at the same time, allow for interim steps we might take."

You are a fool, Reed thought. Don't you realize that Malavy's ridiculous idea that the U.S. find and return Pol Pot to Cambodia for a trial is the only leverage we currently have with him? Malavy would look like a hero to his followers. And the president needed his good offices—for at least the next three months.

"With those rumors rampaging through Cambodia, how stable is the country?" Reed certainly didn't want to do anything that might destabilize the area.

"There is no evidence that the military will attempt a coup. Everyone seems happy about the signing of the treaty except the KR, of course."

"What about the security forces?"

"You mean the one run by the minister of Interior Security?"

"Yes."

"There is no evidence that either his police or paramilitary are mobilizing in any way."

"How reliable are your sources?" Reed knew he would be uncomfortable with the answer, no matter what it was. The one truth about Cambodia, no matter who ruled it, king or dictator, was that there was always an internal movement of troops going from one part of the country to another part to suppress some sort of uprising.

"We check our intel with the Aussies and the Kiwis as a routine matter, since both Australia and New Zealand have more serious national security interests in Cambodia than we do."

"Yes, of course," Reed replied. He knew better. The United States had the greatest national security interests in Cambodia because they needed Cambodia, Vietnam, and Thailand to be politically stable and pro-American.

He stood up and walked over to the world map pinned to his wall. The treaty that the president had pushed Cambodia into signing was working. The United States was already applying political, economic, and military pressure on China to halt its attempt to dominate Southeast Asia directly and indirectly. Over the past few years the U.S. had been successful in obtaining cooperation agreements from the Union of Myanmar (Burma), Thailand, Laos, Vietnam, Taiwan, Malaysia, Indonesia, and the Philippines. And now Cambodia had signed! Malavy's price to join had been the return of Pol Pot. So as long as Pol Pot remained on the loose, the future stability of his government remained questionable and any new growth of the Khmer Rouge within Cambodia could cause disaster in the entire area. All it would take was renewed instability for the sleeping giant, China, to awaken with a vengeance against all these insubordinate countries. Worst of all, the United States would be in no position to do anything.

"I'll consider your suggestion." Reed walked over to the door, signaling that the meeting was over. Then he went to his desk and picked up the telephone. "We need to talk," he said when the ringing on the other side was answered. "How fast can you get over here?"

24

Atherton detested walking the candy-striped hallways of the seventh floor of the State Department. His only pleasure lay in the fact that his identification card gave him access to almost any restricted area in the U.S. government. No one could stop him from entering a military installation or a civilian intelligence operation.

More important than the ID he possessed, however, was the power he wielded without having to demonstrate it. Only a few men in government ever have this type of power. One was his predecessor, Marshal Andrews, who still remained in the bowels of the Pentagon. This seventy-six-year-old lanky gentleman was the creator of the greatest technological incubator of all time—DARPA—Defense Advanced Research Projects Agency—an agency that spawned the GPS (Geographical Positioning Satellite), the DARPA NET (which became the Internet), satellite technology used for medical use, and countless other civilian products.

Atherton was proud of the fact that he came from the DARPA heritage to create the "virtual assassination" unit, located everywhere and nowhere. But he bemoaned the fact that almost everything DARPA created had become commercialized, including his own unit. My God, he thought, as he walked past pasty-faced men in pinstripe suits, how unfairly these poor creatures have been treated throughout the decades. When George Marshall was secretary of state, the Foreign Service was a profession of which one could be proud. Today it was a repository of political correctness, which had no relation to competency. The secretary of state, as well as thirty percent of all ambassadors, were political appointments.

What this meant to Atherton, a government employee of four decades, was that the Foreign Service was at the mercy of amateurs who were supposed to, by some mysterious process, learn and exercise diplomatic skills in three months that it took a professional diplomat twenty years to acquire. As he walked past the bank of secretaries guarding the secretary of state's office, he wondered what would happen if everyone who had a hip replacement decided that he was qualified to become a hip surgeon.

The idea of the patient becoming the doctor riled Atherton, not only because the phenomenon was occurring in the State Department, but because it was also occurring in the Department of Defense. DOD was beginning to outsource war. And the longer he thought about the problem, the more he realized that he could be seen as part of it. The unit he had created was simply an outgrowth of a trend he had anticipated.

Passing Reed's secretary, who greeted him with a warm "hello," he realized that his little creation was in jeopardy if Carter continued to act in a dysfunctional manner. He was certain that the ensuing discussion with Reed would concern the Khmer Rouge problem. There was no doubt in Atherton's mind that news of failure in this assignment would soon be known in the highest circles. Then it would simply be a matter of time before some knownothing bureaucrat, who knew nothing with great certainty, made an "inadvertent" innuendo to a congressman or senator that there were paid assassins acting on behalf of the U.S. government. One or two complaints like those to the House Intelligence Oversight Committee and Atherton's unit would be history. And so would he. As he walked into Reed's office he realized that this was going to be a zero-sum game. He either would be merely reprimanded for what Carter had not done or . . .

"Welcome, Lord Atherton," Reed walked to the door and warmly shook Atherton's hand. He enjoyed teasing Atherton; it was a comfortable comradery.

"And how are the hoi polloi doing?" Atherton walked toward the couch and sat down.

"Anything to drink?" Reed opened a bottle of Cutty Sark without waiting for a response and poured it into two glasses bearing the seal of the State Department.

"No ice, please!" Atherton looked around the spacious office, never tiring of viewing the endless number of autographed photographs of Reed standing alongside different secretaries of state and two presidents. The messages written on each tried to convey a genuine sense of personal gratitude, but as all government employees knew, meant very little, if anything. "To Tom, without whom none of this would have been possible." "To a dear friend and trusted colleague." "Working with you on the treaty was an extraordinary experience." Whether or not Tom really had done something special for each photo-op buddy, Atherton was impressed by the sheer number of photographs and the fact that Reed needed to display them.

"No ice means that you're here to discuss something serious."

"I thought you were the one who called me," Atherton responded. Who called whom was a game of one-upmanship that they always played with each other.

"My sources tell me that we are having problems with our KR problem." Tom sat close to Atherton and spoke in almost a whisper.

"I guess you could say Carter screwed up. Did you have this room swept recently?"

"Why, do you see any cockroaches?" Reed laughed.

"You know exactly what I mean!" Atherton took security matters quite seriously and could never understand Reed's cavalier attitude toward it.

"Routine debugging."

"Once a year?"

"If that." Reed paused. It was time to be direct. "What's the status of our venture? Has he been found yet?"

"To put it simply, no."

"That's not the answer I was hoping to hear. Malavy is waiting for us to return the man back to his native land. The man upstairs is waiting for word of his death. And you tell me that you're nowhere close to concluding your assignment." He leaned even closer to Atherton. "Your concern is nice, but it doesn't give me confidence."

"Does the secretary of state know about Carter?" Atherton asked.

"More importantly"—Reed deflected the question with another question—"did Carter deal with the problem?"

"No. Not yet. He wants to retire from the assignment."

"I don't think that will be possible," Reed stated

matter-of-factly. "It's too late. The clock is running. I know how long it takes to plan an assignment like the one you gave Carter."

"We could try to finesse the next few months, and reiterate our information that Pol Pot had in fact died and that the pictures of his death were real."

"We could, as you say, but we won't. This job has to be done, and done right. Too many people have too much to lose if it's screwed up, as you say Carter might have done."

"I understand," Atherton responded contritely, feeling his own vulnerability. Damn Carter, he thought to himself. "How much time do I have?"

"Two or three weeks," Reed answered, "before the president's campaign kicks into high gear. If Pol Pot surfaces on his own, there's no telling what damage he can do."

"Say no more. Consider it done."

"I'm glad we're in agreement. The man must not return to his country. Do whatever you need to. Even if it means that you undertake the assignment yourself."

"At my age?" Atherton laughed.

"Then join a sports club and get fit. One way or another, everything must be concluded by next month. If not—"

"Je vous comprends!" Atherton interrupted in French. He didn't want to hear a threat from his old friend and colleague. He already could smell the stench of blood.

25

BRONX, NEW YORK

On this twentieth anniversary of Pure Aggression, the cockfight named after the generic form of Speed Strychnine, Yetta Rovner, the attractive, moon-faced, eighty-five-year-old "hostess" of cockfighting for over fifty years, had decided to organize the yearly event in the basement of one of her apartment buildings in the Bronx. A palette of people, cars, and apparel appeared at 10 P.M. in front of the building as if it was the opening night of a movie in Los Angeles in the 1950's. Each of the two hundred attendees brought with him a specific invitation for this illegal and bloodiest of ani-

mal sports. Yetta estimated that over forty percent
of her customers were Asian: Chinese, Thai, Vietnamese, and a sizeable contingency of Cambodians. She knew most of them by name, although
occasionally an invited client appeared in tow with
an unknown guest. What Yetta liked most about the
cockfights was not the fight itself, but the festive,
multi-ethnic atmosphere and the adrenaline everyone brought to the evening.

Yetta was in charge of an entire empire of cockfighting merchandise, clubs, magazines, and events
and she took her responsibilities seriously. She organized cockfighting classes, developed instruc-
tional videos, and published books and newsletters.
Cockfighting, the thirty-two-year-old monthly magazine had twenty thousand subscribers and over one
hundred advertisements aimed at cockfighter devotees.

Yetta greeted all her friends in her inimitable
Yiddish accent—everyone from the blue-blooded
breeders from Connecticut to the chicken farmers
of Delaware. They all knew that she was not only a
pro, but also extremely generous with her awards.
Cock winners received five thousand dollars.
Untested cocks were offered five hundred to enter
their first fight. To every winner's mother hen, Yetta
offered one hundred dollars just for having been a
mother.

But the other side of her cockfighting empire
was somewhat more nefarious. This pleasant, wizened grandmother was also a shrewd, coldblooded

businesswoman who had developed an empire worth over one billion dollars, primarily by selling a panoply of manufactured goods. Her most popular items were the gaffs (metal spurs) and a wide variety of curved, razor-sharp knives, up to three inches long, for mounting on the cocks' legs. Yetta had developed a costly, but popular knife which killed faster than the cheaper gaffs; she designed them so that the knives would rip the flesh of the cock rather than slit it apart. It made the fights unusually bloody.

Conducting business in New York, Yetta had to be well-connected with the office of the mayor of the city. The local Democratic machinery could count on her for significant financial support in local and statewide elections. The precinct police were "greased" to turn their attention away from the apartment buildings she owned and "used" in the neighborhood.

Yetta watched the familiar faces of her customers stream into the building, greeting one with a curt bow, another with a warm handshake. Her arrangement with the neighborhood police assured her that demonstrators who protested her business practices by screaming obscenities at her clientele would be restrained and, if needed, hauled off to overnight lockup for disturbing the peace. It always amazed Yetta how effective several cases of Cutty Sark at Christmas could be.

Some of her grandchildren were running pieces of the empire she had created, breeding birds across the country. The cocks were then sold to people in states where cockfighting was legal, as well as to the Philippines, Guam, Mexico and other countries where the sport was popular. In states where the sport was outlawed the birds were hustled into wooded areas and urban back alleys for illicit combat. Other relatives owned companies which produced and distributed the vitamin- and nutrient-enriched feed for fighting cocks.

In the last few years, however, cockfighting had become a target of animal rights advocates who called the sport barbaric and cruel. They pointed to the banning of dog fighting decades before, and the precedent that was set. Only two years before, the Humane Society of the United States had helped opponents of cockfighting in Arizona and Missouri win ballot initiatives that ultimately outlawed the sport. Earlier in the year the Oklahoma Coalition Against Cockfighting, with financing from the Humane Society, had gathered more than one hundred thousand signatures for a referendum on a proposal to ban the fights and punish violators with fines of up to a hundred thousand dollars and jail terms of twenty years.

Yetta was nobody's fool. This might be one of her last major events. The beginning of the end. Perhaps she had another two more good years in the business. Then she would sell it to the boys from Las Vegas. Her relatives would be free to make their own deals. But she had made a conscious decision not to worry about the future. The best thing to do now was to enjoy what she had, her customers and the game.

"Dr. Allison Carter," Yetta said to the familiar face as she hugged him. "It's been a long while since I've seen you."

"It's been only one year," he responded, clearly cheered by her warmth and now certain that he had made the right decision to leave D.C. for this event.

"One year is at least ten months too many for you to be away from me and the games," she said in mocking reprimand.

"I'm glad to be here," he said in all candor. Rock and roll concerts and cockfights were the only two events he could attend to get himself out of a psychological funk. He had specifically come to Pure Aggression to get out his anger at Atherton. No one, including Atherton, threatened him with impunity. But there was little Carter could do about his feelings of resentment and vulnerability except attend the sport he enjoyed most. Carter had attended several illegal cockfights during his teenage years. But it was in Vietnam that he became addicted to the sport, getting great joy out of seeing different species of cocks indigenous to the Southeast Asian region rip each other to shreds with the panoply of weapons provided. After Vietnam, Carter broke the monotony of overseas assignments by finding out from local bartenders where the nearest cockfight was being held.

"*Boychick*," Yetta said in her best Yiddish inflection, "you look very tired. Is something wrong?"

She had never asked him what he did for a living, but she knew from his self-contained, laconic manner that whatever he did was his own business and not for public consumption. Unlike most of her clients here today, she recognized that he was not simply seeking a vicarious thrill by watching the birds fight. Carter was there for the opposite reason—to purge himself of whatever violence was within him. She sensed that he attended her cockfights for the same reason she would attend synagogue on Yom Kippur, to atone for her sins. For most of her customers, the thrill of the fight was an adrenaline rush. But for Carter, the cockfights had some sort of curative psychological effect. He rarely rooted for any specific bird. He simply placed his bet and then remained transfixed as the birds fought to the death.

"You're a smart woman." Carter truly liked and admired her for her perspicacity, business acumen, and discretion.

"If you were my son," she added, "I would tell you to find a beach and stay there for a couple of weeks, thinking only about how to acquire a nice tan."

"I burn easily," Carter laughed, "but what's real enjoyment without having the opportunity to see you at least once a year?"

"You make an old lady feel girlish." She stood on her toes and kissed him on the forehead.

"Which one of the cocks do you think will win?" he asked, knowing that she wouldn't answer him. In a business without ethics or morality, she had plenty of both. "The Hatch breed or the Round-head?"

"I'll give you one tip, but you have to keep it a secret!"

"I promise!"

"I can guarantee that one of those two cocks will win."

"I think that my welcome has been exhausted," he responded.

"Go inside, before you miss the event!"

"Take care, Yetta!" Carter bent down and kissed her on both cheeks.

"If I were younger," she added, "I certainly wouldn't be kissed there."

As Carter stepped into the elevator going to the basement, someone pushed him from behind.

"I'm so sorry," the hunched-over man apologized. "I've become a bit awkward in my old age."

"That's all right," Carter responded, "no harm was intended."

The old man smiled with the wisdom of the ages as both men walked down a urine-smelling corridor toward the basement arena.

"Enjoy the fights!" the older man said as they parted.

"Thank you, sir," Carter responded. "I hope you do, too."

"I'm certain I will," the old man replied, "I believe there will be a lot of surprises in this game."

"I hope so," Carter's voice trailed off as he entered into the crowd.

"I'm certain you will," Sonn Senn muttered to himself. With Carter here, this would become an event with incalculable benefits for everyone.

26

"Five C notes on Roundhead," a fat man yelled out, holding up a thick stack of dollars, one among dozens of spectators yelling out numbers and waving fistfuls of bills. The fat man ignored the others and simply raised his hand higher in the air and increased his volume.

"Three hundred on the Hatch, and I'll spot you five big ones," Carter shouted. He was seated in the front row of five concentric circles, each circle slightly elevated by a cheap, folding aluminum stand. In the bullpit two men, one in a red baseball cap, the other wearing a gray T-shirt, began the precombat ritual of holding their birds and thrusting them back and forth aggressively at each other.

Yetta always gave Carter a preferential front-row seat. She was the type of person who never forgot a favor. Several years before, at a cockfight in which the crowd was unusually unruly, a fistfight had broken out. While Yetta's security guards were unable to break up the ever-enlarging number of fighters, Carter managed to subdue the man who had started the fight by applying pressure with his hands on the man's neck. The fighting stopped and Yetta had never forgotten what Carter had done. From then on he received a front-row seat at each fight. In return, Carter had learned to adore this tough old bird for the gratitude she had shown to him. Every Mother's Day he would send her a card that would read something along the lines, "To the woman who has always put excitement in my life and worried about me as if she were my mother." From time to time Yetta would send him a greeting card, expressing concern for his health and safety, just like any Jewish mother might do for one of her children.

"Fifty on the red hat!" someone shouted amidst the cacophony of sounds.

"Seventy on the gray T-shirt!" an Asian man shouted back, but kept his eyes on Carter.

The referee, dressed completely in black shouted, "Ready, pit!" Both birds exploded from their handlers' grasps and collided breast to breast, a foot off the ground. Beak grabbing beak, hackles flaring like porcupine quills, they collided and bounced apart again and again. The Hatch took command, ripping a large piece of skin from the Roundhead. Then the Roundhead pounded the Hatch with his foot, piercing and slowly ripping through the Hatch's lung. Spurting blood, piercing shrieks, flying feathers, and ripped flesh created an atmosphere of impending death. Barely alive, both birds continued to lunge at each other for several minutes. But it soon became clear that the denouement of the contest would be binary. One bird would be dead; one bird would be alive. Paralyzed, maimed, or handicapped victims were alien to this type of aggression. The audience expected to witness death. For many viewers, it did not even matter whose. The money bet was, for many, an excuse to root for a kill.

"Fascinating sport," Sonn Senn said to Carter. "A choreography of death."

Carter did not respond. When he was watching a fight he found any tangential comments both intrusive and annoying. He watched as the Hatch seemed to fade, refusing to budge after receiving a major tear in his neck from the Roundhead. But as the Roundhead approached the Hatch for what should have been the final time, the Hatch jumped up and with his two-inch steel gaff ripped the Roundhead's scalp wide open, splattering blood and brain matter all over the pit.

Everyone cheered, including Carter. The odds had changed. The Hatch had been identified from the start as the underdog, so to speak, but now the

Roundhead struck back with his gaff, ripping the initial hole in the Hatch's neck even larger.

"Goddamn it!" Carter shouted at the man in the gray T-shirt who had handled the Hatch. "Get the Hatch out of the way." Carter wasn't worried about his bet. It just bothered him that the Hatch was not being properly managed. There was no strategy for attack and retreat.

"You certainly are a man of passion!" Senn said to Carter with a wry smile.

Carter looked at the wizened Asian face in disgust. He would have liked to tell him to fuck off but said nothing.

Just as Carter suspected, the Hatch faded back, hunkered down in a corner of the pit, and did not move. He started to cough up small chunks of blood. His breathing sounded like footsteps on gravel. The Roundhead, severely wounded, was announced the winner by the referee and both birds were carried from the pit. The audience cheered. Carter ripped up his ticket and paid the fat man.

"I see that you don't mind losing," Senn said, as he watched Carter's every move. "I like someone who knows how to lose with grace."

"What in God's name was so graceful about my losing?" Carter asked brusquely, unable to ignore the man's comments any longer. "There is an old axiom of betting that I learned when I first started playing the cockfights: 'Don't gloat, don't pout! Just take the money or walk away.'" Next time, he thought, he'd choose his seat more carefully.

"Most people dislike losing," Senn responded, "but you do not seem upset."

"Meaning what?" Carter asked, transforming his exasperation to annoyance with a twist of curiosity. Clearly, this old man was going out of his way to establish a dialogue with him. But why?

"Losing tests a man's character. From what I have seen of you, I would say that you are quite strong."

"Now that you've flattered me sufficiently," Carter pursued, "what is it that you want?"

"Simply to talk to you. Is that so unusual?"

"At a cockfight beneath an apartment building in the Bronx," Carter responded, "any discussion other than about a bet or a bird is unusual." Another set of cocks were being brought into the pen. The noise of the crowd had not abated. The excitement of a new fight rushed through Carter's veins, but he decided to sit this fight out and talk to the old man. Something about him, perhaps his composure, his self-assurance, was compelling.

"I come here to watch the cockfights," Senn continued as if Carter had asked him a question, "because they remind me about the thin veneer of civility that covers most of human nature. Quite frankly, the only difference between us and those trained fighting birds is that we do not need any training to kill one another. Nor any Pure Aggression."

"That's quite a cynical view of mankind."

"Many of my friends have accused me of having

a cynical streak. But despite whatever cynicism I may have, the truth is that man is nothing but an animal whose very nature is pure and simple aggression."

"Your point, sir?" Man's aggressive nature was no great secret. So what was the old man trying to tell him, Carter wondered.

"For the most part, man's aggression is hidden, never as directly manifested as we have seen here tonight."

"And . . ."

"Man has a tendency to rationalize his aggression through a variety of expedient disciplines as religion, nationalism, and economics—"

"I think I get the point," Carter interrupted. "I have this disturbing feeling that you are trying to tell me in the most circuitous way something that you feel that I should know."

"Very good, Dr. Allison Carter," Senn said. "Rationalization is a highly underappreciated psychological mechanism."

"I seem to be at a disadvantage. Have we met before? If I'm Dr. Allison Carter, then who might you be?"

"You see," Senn responded, "that's precisely what I was talking about. Instead of directly confronting you at the very beginning, I had to beat around the bush, as you Americans so quaintly say."

"And how long will you continue to play this annoying game of—"

"Oh, please, Dr. Carter," Senn interrupted, "I had no intention of confusing or annoying you. But please take into account my age . . ."

"Then let's talk turkey, as we Americans quaintly say," Carter mockingly replied. "What do you want, Mr. . . . ?"

"Mr. Sonn Senn. I presume that you have heard my name before today's pleasant encounter."

"As a matter of fact, Mr. Senn, I haven't."

"Have you ever made the acquaintance of a young man named Haing Chev?"

Carter shuddered visibly. He felt a sickness start to rise from the pit of his stomach. Had Chev lived longer, Carter decided, he might have brought up Sonn Senn's name.

"Haing Chev," Senn continued, "was an extremely talented young man who met an untimely death at the hands of an unusually skillful assassin."

"If you are referring to me, Mr. Senn, then as you mentioned before it would be best that you confront me directly. So the question remains, Mr. Senn," Carter tried to penetrate Senn's inscrutable stare "what is it that you want from me?"

"Perhaps the question is phrased incorrectly, Dr. Carter," Senn responded boldly. "Maybe the question should be what you may want from me?"

"As far as I know, there is absolutely nothing that I want from you."

"In the long run you might be completely correct. But that is taking a very large gamble."

"You said that you admired the way that I am able to take rejection—"

"—and the way you are able to make calculated risks and stick by your losses," Senn interrupted. "Those are truly honorable traits."

"So what is it that you want?"

"Please be assured that I did not follow you here to accuse a distinguished State Department physician of first-degree murder."

"Your point, Mr. Senn?" Carter was getting nervous. This man knew far too much about him. How he had gotten his information? From whom? And for what purpose?

"Think of what it is that you might need from me, instead of making yourself the center of attention, Dr. Carter. You and I are connected through many channels."

"Let's not be coy, Mr. Senn. You seem to know who I am and what I've done. Haing Chev's death was an unfortunate accident. It is one that will haunt me all of my life. But I assure you, it will never happen again. I am now on vacation—permanent vacation."

"I have been informed that you were ordered to infiltrate Cambodian refugee groups that have members of the Khmer Rouge."

"I can't confirm that!"

"Please, Dr. Carter," Senn responded firmly, "any protests on your part would diminish my respect for you." He continued slowly, for emphasis. "Your ultimate objective is . . . or was . . . to find and kill Pol Pot, the alleged leader of the Khmer Rouge in the United States." Senn paused for dramatic appeal. "Would it interest you to know that some people presume that I am Pol Pot?"

"At this point, I'm not really interested in who you are. The fact is that you are now completely irrelevant to my life, whether you are 'presumed' as you say, to be Pol Pot, Hitler, Stalin, or Mao Tsetung." Carter hoped his reaction seemed truthful to Senn. In fact, Carter didn't know how he felt about Senn's revelation. It had come too fast. Carter hadn't had enough time to process it. He paused, suddenly weary. He had hoped that this excursion to New York would take his mind off his problems. But here they were, sitting beside him. "Unless you are in the American Foreign Service and have some malady, I am not concerned about you or your problems. Period! It's as simple as that, Mr. Senn, or whoever you might or might not be!" Carter started to feel anxious, wondering how many other spectators were there accompanying the old man. And what their plans were for him.

"I'm afraid that General James Atherton has different ideas!" Senn shouted after Carter as he watched him depart to the noise of a bloodcurdling cheer from the crowd.

27

Carter and Senn walked outside of the building into
the quiet, dark sidewalk. When Senn, and what
probably were his bodyguards, had appeared at his
side in the elevator, Carter realized that there was no
way that Senn wasn't going to be heard. Atherton,
no doubt, was playing games with both of them, although Carter wasn't sure which game it was. Now
he understood how this old man knew so much
about him. It wouldn't even surprise Carter if Atherton put Pol Pot, himself, on the payroll! I might as
well make the most of the conversation, Carter concluded. "You told me that I might need you."

"That's correct!" Sonn Senn moved slowly. The two strapping bodyguards following them had no trouble maintaining the appropriate distance. The weapons hidden beneath their jackets, however, couldn't be more obvious.

"What did you mean by that?" Carter asked.

"General Atherton is a very clever man," Senn answered, "but he is only a tool of some very senior officials in your government."

"And where does a vacationing physician come into all of this?"

"Come now, Dr. Carter, this is not the time to be coy. Your reputation precedes you as a man who wants questions answered immediately and answers explained even faster."

"Mark if off as an American trait." Carter couldn't help but smile. The Asian, he thought, certainly lived up to Atherton's standards. He had done his homework. He was deliberate, clever, enigmatic . . . but painfully slow.

"I have excused your apparent indifference to me on the grounds that you have suffered severe emotional strains recently due to . . . ineptness, shall we say?"

"Thank you for the gratuitous insult." Carter wondered whether the old man was referring to Chev's death or whether he knew anything about his job on the Vineyard. Carter looked behind him as they walked, watching the bodyguards visually scan the streets and rooftops.

"Sometimes the young cub must be reigned in for his own benefit."

"Please, don't patronize me, Mr. Senn." Carter had no desire to hear anything that would complicate his life. And he certainly didn't need to be lectured to by someone whose past might be more scandalous than his own.

"I think it best that we continue our conversation somewhere else." Sonn Senn turned around, nodded to his bodyguard, and a black Cadillac limousine with dark tinted windows seemed to appear out of nowhere. The bodyguards rushed immediately to take their usual positions, holding the rear doors open for both Sonn Senn and Carter. The car pulled away just as some spectators from the cockfight emerged from the apartment building.

"Where are we going?" Carter asked the question seriously but really didn't expect an answer. A cat-and-mouse game had begun, and for the first time, Carter was going to be the one learning how to squeak.

"As you Americans like to say," Senn responded with a broad smile, "relax and leave the driving to us."

"So, are we going to play doctor-held-hostage-meets-chinese-fortune-cookie-philosopher?"

"I don't quite understand what that means," Senn responded, "but I know you to be a man of sharp wit and not one who would tolerate fools easily."

"Quite frankly, I don't like that trait in me,"

Carter offered, wondering just how much this guy did know about him. Carter couldn't wait to have a long talk with Atherton. A lot needed to be explained. "It tends to make me appear more cynical than I really am." He paused, wondering why he was bothering to respond to Senn's circuitous innuendos. The thought had occurred to him that the result of their "conversation," as Senn had called it, could be a bullet in the head for Carter. If Senn knew about Haing Chev and Atherton, he could be trying to extract as much information from Carter as he could, before the kill. But if Senn was out to neutralize him, why would he go to such great lengths to acquaint himself with Carter? And if Senn was really Pol Pot . . .

Carter looked at his watch. They had been in the car for about twenty minutes. Although the tinted windows didn't allow him to see outside, at one point he heard the exchange of money in the front seat between the chauffeur and what was probably an attendant at a tollbooth.

"I sense a certain tension in your body," Senn commented after a few minutes of silence.

"Put yourself in my position, Mr. Whoever-you-are." Carter's voice conveyed the fatigue he felt. "I don't know who you are, although you seem to know a lot about me, which generally isn't a very healthy state for me to be in. You planned a 'chance' meeting for both of us and then forced me, with a velvet-glove approach, into a car driven by killers for hire, headed to an unknown location."

"A point well taken," Senn laughed, something he rarely did in front of a caucasian. He didn't expect Carter to be so honest with his feelings. Was Carter trying to manipulate him in some way? He was almost ready to believe that Carter really had no further interest in Atherton's assignment.

"Would it be presumptuous of me to ask you where you are taking me?" Carter's bleak mood changed with Senn's laugh. The tension between them was starting to diminish. Perhaps they really weren't working at cross purposes.

"Since we share the enjoyment of a sport that involves risk, combat, and survival," Senn responded, "I think that you will find the place to which I am taking you quite interesting."

"It sounds as if we are going to either a poultry slaughterhouse or a horror film."

"I enjoy your sense of humor, Dr. Carter."

"I'm glad that we share another common bond," Carter responded, "macabre humor."

"Dr. Carter, I would like to assure you that if you were to fear for your life, now is not the time."

"Does that mean you will inform me when I should start worrying?"

"You will recognize it yourself."

"Which means that it won't be very subtle."

"Precisely," Senn continued. "Anyway, I think that you will be pleasantly surprised. But you must be patient."

"Do I have a choice?"

"Not at all," Senn responded. "So let us think of

the time we are spending together as a valuable experience for two individuals from two different cultures, trying to find a common ground in which they can work together."

"I'm infatuated with the 'work together' part," Carter responded. "What are you suggesting?"

"I know that you were sent to find and kill Pol Pot." Senn's tone of voice took a serious turn. He was no longer smiling or laughing. "But the real mystery that you and I should solve together is why Pol Pot is in the United States after he was declared an international war criminal by every country represented at the International War Crimes Tribunal at The Hague."

"Except for the United States," Carter corrected. "We never condemned him."

"We are now thinking as one," Senn concluded. "And now you must ask yourself why Pol Pot's . . . associates . . . who killed thousands of innocent Cambodians, were allowed to settle in the United States and live peacefully here behind a newly created identity."

"As far as I know, there was a great humanitarian outcry in this country to do something for the displaced Cambodians who claimed political asylum. Everyone helped sponsor the refugees. The churches. The synagogues. Relatives living in the U.S. And lots of documents were checked before they were given visas to enter the United States— and assistance from social agencies."

"I am disappointed, Dr. Carter. Do you always believe what you read?"

"You couldn't turn on your television set without witnessing some family tragedy that cried for America to open its door to the refugees." Carter didn't like feeling defensive. Especially for an act of kindness and generosity on the part of America. "That's our country's tradition," he continued. "It's what makes America different. We are a melting pot." He hoped he didn't sound trite to Senn, but this is how he had always felt about the country which had given him the opportunity to be anything he wanted to be.

"Would you believe me if I told you that pure politics and simple greed governed who came into your country, and not some idealized notion of compassion or humanitarianism?"

Carter looked at Senn as if he were seeing him for the first time. The old man knew things that he didn't. But sounded like he should.

"Would you believe an old Cambodian—already under suspicion of being Pol Pot—that a handful of documents in the possession of my community, which are duplicates of those held as classified documents by your State Department, could destroy the career of many of your superiors?"

"I guess that if I did believe you, I'd want to see those documents for myself." Carter threw out the challenge.

"Just as I hoped," Senn responded. "Shall we go?"

28

"The news is not good," Reed stated nervously to the silver-haired man sitting opposite him. "So far, the general has not been able to deliver on any part of the mission."

"On any part?" Secretary of State S. H. Richards asked. His quiet questioning belied an aggressive, sadistic manner that was known and feared throughout the department. Tall and heavy, his presence in a room seemed to displace both mass and space. No one who knew better made the mistake of trying to get close to him. His highly intellectualized ap-

proach to problems and people belittled anyone who
dared question him.

"No, sir," Reed responded. "It's been several
weeks since the assignment was given to Atherton,
who then subcontracted it to Allison Carter." He
was going to say something more but he knew that
Richards did not like someone who said any more
than he had to. Reed had been warned by several
colleagues that he talked too much and that the secretary found it annoying.

"Dr. Carter?" Richards's curiosity was piqued.
"The one who works in Med?" As they spoke,
Richards meticulously cleaned his fingernails with
a metal nail file, a clear sign of contempt. Reed
waited patiently, his eyes wandering around the el-
egant room in which eighteenth-century desks, ar-
moires, and chairs constituted the decor. How the
hell did Richards know this already, he asked himself, wondering what other surprises were in store
for him if this was only the start of the meeting. In
this small world of the gray zone of national security there were surprisingly countless ways of obtaining information. Richards might even have
gone to the very sources themselves—Atherton and
Carter—and was just giving Reed a hard time.

"Yes, the very same one." Reed wanted to say
how competent Carter had been in past assignments
but decided, again, to say nothing more unless
asked.

"Am I mistaken," Richards asked, "or have I
been misinformed about Dr. Carter resigning from

the assignment? As well as any further ones." He replaced the nail file in his breast pocket, leaned back in his wing-back chair, and placed his size-eleven feet on the glass coffee table. The soles of his shoes were directly facing Reed.

"Well . . ." Reed was at a loss for words.

"Well, what?" Richards asked with an impatient edge to his voice.

"Yes, everything you just said was correct."

"So why does it seem so inane?" Richards tried to control his anger, but knew he hadn't succeeded. He removed his feet from the table and leaned forward toward Reed. "You had Atherton assign a professional to a delicate mission who was reluctant to take the assignment? Then several weeks later, you come here to tell me that with only a few months before the election—need I remind you that we both work for the man—you have not been able to find the man who could lose the election for the president, cost me my job, and certainly discredit your years of service as an FSO?" Richards stood and loomed over Reed. "Where the hell is Pol Pot?"

Beads of sweat were forming on Reed's forehead, most unusual for a man considered affectionately by his peers as the unflappable Englishman of the State Department.

"May I ask a stupid question?"

"Of course!" Reed realized that he was not finished with being the object of derision.

Richards sat and tried to calm down. Unfortunately, his neck remained bright red, betraying his

real emotions. "If Dr. Carter did not want to undertake the assignment, weren't there other professionals who could have, with alacrity and enthusiasm?"

"Unfortunately, I don't have that answer," Reed
responded, unable to look straight into Richards's
piercing blue eyes.

"Why don't you have that answer?" Richards
could feel his heart pounding loudly. He had to convince himself not to strangle Reed or hastily pro-
nounce the words, *you're fired!* when, in fact, his
FSO status made him invulnerable.

"Mr. Secretary," Reed said in a plaintive voice,
"we messed up!"

"We?"

"I screwed up!" Reed suddenly realized that the
secretary's desultory questioning was directed toward one purpose—Reed's admission of culpabil-
ity.

"Then what do you intend to do about it?"
Richards asked. Confession was not enough. He
needed to extract more.

"What would you like me to do?" Reed took out
his handkerchief and wiped his sweaty face. He
knew that he was in a no-win situation.

"I think you know the answer without my having
to tell you." Richards started to raise his massive
frame from the chair, angling his back into position
as he stood upright.

"I see that you still have that infernal back problem," Reed commented, hoping to bring back some
collegiality to the meeting.

Richard ignored the concern. He walked slowly and painfully to his mahogany desk and rested against it. "Do everything necessary to accomplish the mission!"

"Everything?" Reed banged his knees against the glass coffee table as he stood up. He smiled to himself. Carter would call hitting his knees Freudian; he had unconsciously punished himself for failing to execute the mission. Damn that Carter, he thought.

"Does the word *everything* offend you in any way?" Richards went to the far side of his desk and sat down in his leather upholstered chair, seeking some respite from the constant back pains he had to endure.

Reed remained silent. He knew what *everything* connoted. It was one of those loaded words.

"Are we then clear about employing whatever methods that you, in your personal judgment, Mr. Reed, deem necessary? That includes using every conceivable weapon in your arsenal, so to speak."

"Mr. Secretary, I can't in good conscience agree fully with your . . . request." Reed knew that Richards was being obscure enough in his words that he could not be considered a co-conspirator. "If you would like me to step aside, right here and now, so that you can give my assignment to someone else, I will do so. You need to have someone whom you completely trust."

"Have I mentioned the word *trust* anywhere, Mr. Reed? Or distrust?"

"No, sir!"

"Then, why are you bringing it up?"

"Because you are asking me to do something that I don't feel comfortable doing!"

"And what might that be?"

"Employing any method necessary to resolve the situation!"

"Perhaps you misunderstood me."

"I don't think so, sir!" Reed was determined to call the secretary of state's bluff. He had worked too long in the State Department not to know that when an ambiguous order had literally deadly implications and, at the same time, allowed the superior to legitimately distance himself from the order. It was his, Reed's, career and reputation that he was placing on the line. While Richards was uniformly perceived as a man of great integrity by the public, Reed knew him to be a coward who would allow himself to be humiliated if he had to, in order to get what he wanted. And he had proven time and time again, over the years, that he had no scruples about distancing himself from his closest friends when it served his political purpose. Reed was not naïve enough to think that there would be no consequences if he turned this assignment down. He already knew too much. So he had no other choice than to play high-stakes poker. He would handle Carter his own way.

"Well, the hell with it!" Richards laughed out loud, as if the mood in the room had always been one of great levity. "I'm not going to lose one of my best undersecretaries over a few misunderstandings of the English language. Do it your own way. Only let's make sure that we all stay employed."

"Thank you, sir!"

They shook hands and Reed exited the secretary of state's office. But Reed was far from counting his blessings. He had just won a no-win game.

Richards paced his office anxiously. As far as he was concerned, Carter was now a loose cannon. Whether or not Carter, or someone else, disposed of Pol Pot, was only one of Richards's concerns. The other one was what Carter might uncover by being on the street. The secretary of state picked up his telephone and ordered his secretary to call a trusted colleague.

29

Richards riffled through one of the many stacks of papers on his desk. No one was going to take away the glory of his accomplishments in Cambodia and Vietnam. Especially not Dr. Allison Carter, technically one of his employees at State. He had wanted to get rid of Carter for a long time, but some bureaucratic, political, or legal impediment would always arise to prevent him from dismissing the man. He seemed to have protectors everywhere, within State, DOD, the CIA, and on the Hill. And Richards was too smart for self-destruction. He was well acquainted with the axiom that if you want to seek revenge you might as well dig two graves. One for your enemy and one for yourself.

Richards's principle concern at this stage in his career was his almost-finished manuscript and its publication after he resigned from his position as secretary of state. This was his tour de force—his one chance at immortality. Signing the Southeast Asian Peace Treaty had been a crowning accomplishment in the final chapters of the book, and possibly of his career. Pol Pot's return to Cambodia would destabilize that country and their participation in the treaty faster than that slimy Malavy could ever hope to put him on trial. It would make a mockery of everything that he, Richards, had done over the last five years to bring peace to the region.

His manuscript's working title said it all: *U.S. Leadership of the Cambodia Settlement.* The book was certain to become a classic in international diplomacy. It could conceivably make him even more famous than his mentor, former Secretary of State Henry Kissinger, who had written several books about his accomplishments during his tenure as both national security advisor and secretary of state—and had received several million dollars for his words. Richards, and a few of Kissinger's former confidantes, felt that whatever Kissinger thought he had accomplished was due more to the vision of his benefactor, former President Richard Nixon. But like Kissinger, Richards knew that he had an extremely difficult time giving credit for professional accomplishments to anyone except himself. But Cambodia was truly his baby. He had spent so much time on Cambodian issues that he had become known informally around State as the Secretary of State for Cambodia, a country which he himself, in private, would admit had little, if any, national security interest for the United States.

He cradled his manuscript in his hands. Its publication would be a dream come true. The book would detail how he, almost single-handedly, had made it possible for the United States and all the other major powers involved in Southeast Asia— Russia, China, Australia, Britain, and France—to exit Cambodia with the country acting like a true democracy. Hadn't democratic elections been held only months ago? The world would know him as a diplomat who had brought peace, democracy, and prosperity to Cambodia. That was in his manuscript and that was what he had accomplished. But if events did not follow that course, if Pol Pot returned to foment riots among the lingering Khmer Rouge, his time would be seen as nothing more than another bureaucrat's "nice try."

His reverie was interrupted by the presence of a handsome middle-aged man in his doorway.

"Come in, John." Richards beckoned him forward.

"Always a pleasure to see you, Mr. Secretary." John Winthrop seated himself in the same chair Reed had just vacated. He was obviously familiar with the office and a friend of the secretary. "I came as soon as you called."

"As you know"—Richards put his manuscript into a desk drawer and walked over to where Winthrop was sitting—"I have always been impressed by your professionalism as chairman of the Business Council of America."

"Thank you, Mr. Secretary," Winthrop responded, "does this mean you need something from me in that capacity?"

Richards smiled, not at all offended by Winthrop's get-to-the-point bluntness. It was that approach to life that had made him successful in business and as a lobbyist. He was known as a "mover and shaker." Richards had known Winthrop for years, and he had never been anything less than effective and discreet. And that was what Richards needed at this very moment.

Winthrop was totally relaxed, waiting to hear what request Richards would make of him. Whatever it was, he would probably find some reason to help him. After many years in Washington, Winthrop had come to the conclusion that there were neither permanent enemies nor permanent friends, only permanent interests. And he certainly represented many business interests on Capitol Hill.

"Something has come up that may adversely affect businesses you represent—a problem I'm having in the system," Richards began.

"And that . . . problem . . . your problem . . . will

affect me?" Winthrop was aware of the code words that a man in Richards's position frequently had to use. They both had to assume that the room was bugged, standard operating procedure in the realm of national security, where everyone had to have a modicum of paranoia.

"May I review any . . . papers . . . to get a better idea of the problem?"

"I have some right here on my desk." Richards pushed himself up from his chair and slowly walked to his desk. He picked up a folder and handed it to Winthrop. "Here are the papers that need to be reviewed. I'll wait while you study them. They can't leave the room." Richards didn't have to spell out the obvious to a pro like Winthrop; the business of foreign affairs is business.

Winthrop's face blanched as he leafed through the documents he had been handed. A gnawing sensation hit him in the pit of his stomach. All he could see by the time he had read, and reread some of the documents was his name being dragged through the press—either before or after he was forced to step down from the Council. "Very interesting," he remarked as he handed the file back to Richards. "I understand why you called me."

"You see why we need to know what Carter is up to. . . . I can't have him find those documents."

30

QUEENS, NEW YORK

Autumn is the cricket-fighting season in all of Southeast Asia, a time when high rollers and insect specialists spend the better part of their days examining little brown bugs that were captured in distant fields, noting obscure physical details and behaviors in an interminable search for the "golden killer."

For the unfamiliar, fighting crickets are not to be confused with household crickets, which are large, colorful insects with especially lovely chirps kept as companions in little cages with ornate gourds. In contrast, fighting crickets are no more than an inch and a half long and, to the novitiate, appear to be a plain brown color. They are always male and must have the physique and mean character to go directly up against another brown, mean, male cricket. The crickets fight inside an eight-inch plastic arena, butting and grabbing and flipping an opponent until it surrenders or is severely maimed.

Cricket matches have been popular in Asia for centuries with both emperors and commoners. Today, the fights are held weekly in back alleys from Queens, New York to Beijing, China. Each October a national championship is held, usually in Shanghai or Beijing.

Like most combative sports, cricket fighting has become increasingly dominated by hard-core gamblers who stage secret matches for monetary stakes that run into the thousands of dollars. More often than not, just like at the Olympics or a horse race, the competing crickets are doped with an herbal medicine that *aficionados* swear makes them more fierce.

"You need to look at the legs and the jaws of this one," Chea Sambath, a heavyset, cherubic-faced man said as he wiped the sweat off his brow.

"What about the straight lines on his head? Doesn't that indicate your cricket may be somewhat less aggressive than you think?" Senn pointed to one particular cricket as he and Carter crouched in the back alley of a predominantly Cambodian neighborhood in Queens.

Carter was no longer anxious. If Senn had

wanted to kill him, they wouldn't be spending these minutes looking at crickets. Whatever Senn really wanted to show him would wait until this old man was ready. Was it possible, Carter asked himself, for any Caucasian to truly understand the Asian concept of time and patience?

Senn looked at Carter and smiled. He noticed that Carter had begun to relax. Maybe after all this was over he would suggest that Carter spend some time with a Cambodian woman of pleasure.

Carter watched the cricket promoters smoke and joke as they put a female cricket in each fighter's jar to stir up its fighting juices. They used a small scale to weigh each fighter, matching up equals for the coming bouts. When the battles began, the crickets would be dropped into the arena, two at a time.

"Do you know that many of these matches end up in a TKO because one cricket refuses to fight?" Senn asked. "They run away even as their master strokes them with a fine brush. The bolder fighters rush at each other ruthlessly, grasping each other with their large jaws, rising up together with their legs extended like two miniature sumo wrestlers. Unlike the cockfights, very often their behavior draws smiles and laughs from the crowd."

"I don't want you to think that I am not appreciative of this lesson . . ." Carter began, hoping to move Senn a little closer to addressing why they were together and where they were going.

"Dr. Carter, note how the crickets twist and flip

their opponents, judo-style, until one of them re-
treats or is declared the loser." Senn wouldn't be
pushed. All things, in their time, was best.

"I don't think that was the answer I was looking
for."

"The winners will fight again another day," Senn
continued, "often as many as five or six times before they have lost their edge." He paused and
looked at Carter. "Losers are unceremoniously
tossed away."

"I know that I am supposed to understand what
you are saying, but . . ." Carter was exasperated
with the endless metaphors involving these stupid
crickets.

"As you can see from the crickets there are different styles of fighting." Senn was clearly ignoring
Carter's plea to speak in a more straightforward
Western style. "A combatant with a strategy of
'creep like a tiger, fight like a snake,' stalks the
enemy slowly at first, and then suddenly rises up to
attack."

"What about confronting a competitor directly
like a bull?" Carter asked, deciding to join Senn in
his cryptic use of the metaphor.

"The force of a fine steed is when it charges like
the wind. But only at the most propitious moment."

"And how successful is that strategy?" Carter
asked, no longer clear about who was the bull, or
the horse, or the cricket. He was definitely out of
his league conceptually. And he had no doubt that
Senn was a brilliant strategist.

"Strategy is what makes a great champion," Senn responded. "I prefer a less direct strategy, one where the cricket listens for the sound of the other cricket, then looks for the cricket, and then ambushes the enemy cricket after having heard it chirp. There are many characteristics that experts of this game look at before they decide on which fighter to bet."

"And what would those traits be?" Carter asked, amused by the way Senn was evading him—yet teaching him.

"The six possible colors of the body and head. The straightness of the 'fighting lines' on the head. The size of the legs and jaws."

"And that's it?" Carter asked.

"Of course, a goodlooking cricket," Senn answered, "must be tested for its aggressiveness as well."

31

Tom Reed was pacing restlessly over his frayed
Persian carpet. He had just been assigned one of
those "special favor" cases from an administrative
assistant to the leading senator on the Senate International Affairs Committee. It seems that a middle-
aged couple had been physically harassed and then
summarily thrown off a Russian train at Brest, Belarus, as it made its way from Moscow to Warsaw,
for no other apparent reason than the fact they were
Americans. The couple had demanded that the president of Belarus, an old-time communist thug, apologize to them through his ambassador to the United

States and apologize to the American government as well. The couple also demanded reparations of twenty thousand dollars, the amount that it cost them to completely reroute their trip from the U.S. back to Warsaw.

This was not the type of work Reed particularly enjoyed. As the Undersecretary for Political Affairs he worked primarily on major foreign policy matters, such as the final signing of the ASEAN Treaty. The only item he really wanted to focus on was the unfinished matter with Prime Minister Malavy. Malavy had been calling him every day since their last meeting in Ankgor Wat to check on whether Pol Pot had been located. Reed knew that as the presidential election drew nearer the calls would change in tone, from a gentle reminder to a veiled threat.

How could Reed be expected to concentrate on important issues when he was being asked to spend it on Belarus, a matter that should have been handled by SCA, Security and Counselor Affairs? That was the bureau that dealt with the everyday problems of American citizens around the world. Of course, for the most part, SCA was known to be ineffectual. But it did serve one very useful function: It provided a convenient cover for covert CIA agents all over the globe. Of course, that cover was no real secret to a professional in any host country, but it made the CIA feel good that, at minimum, their people could say that they worked for the State Department. So every time Reed would try to reassign a special case back to SCA, it would magically reappear on his desk. That was the bureaucratic way that the CIA paid back State for having to take on crap work in order to maintain its cover.

What in God's name was he supposed to do about a couple thrown off a train in the middle of the night in Belarus, he wondered. He could order one of his ambassadors to make a *demarche*, a written protest, to the president of Belarus. But what would that accomplish? If the president were shrewd, which he was, he would accept responsibility for the transgression and inform the U.S. Ambassador that he would reprimand the border guards for their inappropriate behavior. But everyone involved knew that this was little more than a charade. In fact, this entire Kabuki of diplomacy was, at best, an accepted ritual of protocol signifying nothing, or very little. Eventually, Reed realized, diplomacy as a statecraft would no longer exist. It would be substituted by "virtual diplomacy," the Internet, or some mechanism where no one had to see each other. In time, he predicted, there would be no need for a secretary of state or even a State Department. Instead, a few people would be assigned to sophisticated computers around the world, transmitting information and transacting the business of diplomacy.

Reed put the Belarus file back in the "pending" box. He had bigger issues to worry about. Since his meeting with Richards he had put word out into the system that he needed to talk with Atherton. That was his only real chance to get hold of Carter. But so far he hadn't heard anything from him.

Reed was also more than a little concerned that the secretary of state no longer trusted him. Didn't Richards remember that they were on the same side? As much as he, Reed, promised Malavy that Pol Pot would be safely returned to Cambodia for trial, both he and Richards knew that Pol Pot wouldn't make it out of America alive, so a lot of things did not make sense to Reed. Richards's anxiety was definitely out of proportion to the current situation. Reed decided he needed some perspective on the situation.

Just as he was reaching for the telephone, it rang. The person on the other end of the line was precisely the one he wanted to contact.

"How are you, Senn? I'm so glad you called."

"I have very little time to talk . . ."

"What can I do for you?"

"The question, my friend, is what are you trying to do to me?"

"What do you mean?" Reed asked disingenuously.

"I have recently made the acquaintance of a Dr. Allison Carter. I think you know him."

"He is a physician here at State, if that's what you are asking about." Reed began to sweat profusely. He was glad that Senn wasn't in the room.

"Dr. Carter did not originally desire to enjoy the cricket matches with me. Who sent him?"

"I believe it was the secretary of state," Reed responded. There was no reason why Senn wouldn't believe that.

"That was a very foolish move."

"I know, but he is quite frustrated. He wants to rid himself of the entire problem."

"Including me?"

"I honestly don't know. But I have no reason to believe so." Reed lied easily on the telephone. But this time even he wasn't sure about what the secretary of state was doing, and why.

"Please do your best to find out whether I am in danger."

"I will be happy to." As Reed hung up the telephone he suddenly realized that the secretary of state was determined to find and kill Pol Pot—whether or not he really existed or whether or not he was even in America. And Sonn Senn might as well be him, for all Richards cared.

Senn hung up the phone and turned to Carter. "This call should make your Mr. Reed quite nervous. Perhaps some of it will get transmitted to your secretary of state. Meanwhile, you and I must find those documents I promised to show you."

Carter smiled. He admired the way Senn could play all sides off against each other. Senn's allegiance would always be a matter of self-interest. The real problem lay with the fact that Sonn Senn's interests were only known to Sonn Senn himself.

32

From the brown brick exterior, the building looked more like an abandoned public elementary school than a Cambodian community center. But once inside the building, the center looked more like a museum than a recreation center. Along a long corridor hung framed black-and-white pictures accompanied by signs in both English and what Carter soon realized was Khmer. As he stopped in front of several pictures, Carter saw that many were of emaciated Cambodians holding a placard with numbers on it against their chests.

"Welcome to Tuol Sleng, the prison where thousands of poor souls were tortured daily and eventually killed." Senn spoke matter-of-factly, having guided many people through these halls.

The pictures went from those of individuals with placards, to individuals in cells, to individuals in rooms containing leather straps, metal chains, and buckets with excrement.

"As you can imagine," Senn continued, "these were some of the implements that Pol Pot and his colleagues used to interrogate their victims."

"And the picture of that pile of shredded clothing?" Carter knew the answer, but wanted to hear not only what Senn would say about it, but how he would say it. The longer he knew Senn, the harder it was for Carter to believe that he could be Pol Pot. But if, in fact, he was Pol Pot, his acting was superb.

"The shredded clothing became a symbol of the people who were slaughtered for nothing more than having owned a dog, or for wearing eyeglasses and looking intellectual, or for having been a teacher, doctor, or any type of professional."

They continued down the dimly lit hallway in silence until Senn stopped before a picture of thousands of human skulls piled one on top of another. While most visitors turned their heads away quickly, Carter was mesmerized by the fact that few of the skulls showed any signs of physical damage. Most of the victims had been decapitated.

Carter had seen this infamous picture several

times before, in journals and in museum exhibits on the Vietnam War. What always impressed him was the fact that to accomplish a genocide, organization and compliance were crucial elements. Carter was not a stranger to death camps. He had visited them in Poland—Treblinka, Auschwitz-Birkenau, Sobibor. Ironically, the sophisticated Nazis and the primitive Cambodians possessed several talents in common. First was the ability to organize large numbers of people and transport them wherever required. Second was the ability to exterminate millions of people without a great outcry from anyone in the world. The Germans had killed close to ten million people—Jews, Christians, gypsies, homosexuals, the mentally retarded, the physically deformed—with very little resistance either from the victims or from the rest of the world, shipping them to Poland from as far away as Greece.

The Nazis had created a formidable killing machine based completely on numbers. How many people could be killed every hour in a crematorium using Zyklon-B gas—twenty thousand per hour? Twenty-five thousand per hour? Numbers were important.

The Khmer Rouge did in their people their own way. They had one million Cambodians walking barefoot from Phnom Penh, the capital of Cambodia, into the jungles of the countryside. Those that made the walk were then butchered by having their throats cut by the sharp edge of the leaves of a palm tree.

Carter had always believed that the rise of Pol Pot could not have happened without President Nixon's direct, personal, and illegal orders to commence saturation bombing of Cambodia during the Vietnam War. He was at wit's end trying to stop the North Vietnamese from utilizing Cambodia as an alternative supply route to that of the Ho Chi Minh Trail. But there were more culprits, many of whom had resurrected themselves after the war as humanitarians. One came to mind immediately—former Secretary of Defense Robert McNamara. A technocrat, considered one of the whiz kids at DOD, he had a strong propensity to lie and an even greater need to cower from direct confrontation regarding his involvement in the Vietnam War.

Then, of course, there was the self-aggrandizing former Secretary of State Henry Kissinger, who had always been concerned about his legacy as the greatest statesman of the twentieth century, writing tomes of books about his incredible diplomatic accomplishments. For Carter, both McNamara and Kissinger should have been tried as war criminals right after the withdrawal of American troops from Vietnam.

"Restraint is an important Asian virtue," Senn whispered to Carter, who he could see was becoming increasingly angry.

"Is this time line depicting key events in the life of Pol Pot correct?" Carter ignored Senn's placating comment, but was interested in a chart in a glass exhibition case in the center of the corridor.

"I believe it is," Senn replied, "I can read it aloud for you, if you wish."

Carter looked quizzically at Senn. There was something either sadistic or masochistic about Senn's wanting to recount, out loud, the history of a heinous killer. Something was very strange, Carter thought. Or was this another one of Senn's lessons which Carter would have to decode for its true meaning?

"Key Events in the Life of Pol Pot—Leader of Cambodia's Khmer Rouge." Senn read the first line with the same concentration as if he were seeing it for the first time.

The Early Years

1925: Saloth Sar, known as Pol Pot, is born in Kompong Thom Province.

1949–1952: Pol Pot wins a government scholarship, goes to Paris to study, becomes a Communist.

1953: Pol Pot returns to Cambodia, joins the Indochinese Communist Party, recruits sympathizers while teaching school.

1954: Cambodia wins independence from France.

1960: Cambodians form their own Communist Party.

Pol Pot Ascends to Power Within the Party

1963: Pol Pot becomes General Secretary of
the Communist Party, flees to the jungle to escape repression by Cambodia's ruler, Prince
Norodom Sihanouk. Pol Pot's identity is
transformed from his original Saloth Sar fea-
tures. No one outside his immediate circle
knows what he looks like.

"So the pictures of his death could be completely
false?" Carter asked.

"Yes!"

"Then how would any Cambodian know whether
someone who claims to be Pol Pot, the leader of the
Khmer Rouge, is really him?" Carter smiled to himself. Was it only a week ago that he was searching for
a man that no one would or could identify so that he
could kill him? All of a sudden Carter felt that he had
been abused—and by his own government. Mission
impossible! Any Cambodian of approximately the
right age could claim to be Pol Pot. Or disclaim to be
him.

"A leader of any ideological movement is easily
recognized by his own people by his charisma, ability to lead, and . . ."

". . . and his ability to be a ruthless killer."

Senn ignored Carter's comment and continued
talking as if he had an audience of hundreds.

1967: Peasants take up arms in Battambang Province to protest a rice tax. The army suppresses the insurrection.

1968: The Khmer Rouge revolts against the government of Prince Sihanouk.

1970: Prince Sihanouk is toppled in a right-wing coup that leads to civil war. Sihanouk joins the Khmer Rouge against the new right-wing leaders in Phnom Penh. The U.S. supports the new government.

1975–1979: The Khmer Rouge seizes power and begins an experiment in agrarian Communism. More than a million Cambodians die from starvation, overwork, and execution.

1979–1990: Pol Pot and the Khmer Rouge are given refuge at the border of Thailand where they fight against Vietnamese invaders of Cambodia.

1991: All Cambodian factions sign a peace agreement.

1993: The Khmer Rouge boycotts a U.N.-supervised election.

The Beginning of the End

August 1996: The newly elected government announces the breakup of the Khmer Rouge.

Pol Pot's brother-in-law, Ieng Sary, leads guerrillas to defect.

June 1997: Pol Pot orders a key aide, Son Sen, and family killed; hard-liners split into two factions.

"Is that Son Sen any relationship to you?" Carter asked.

"No," Senn replied, "the name is spelled many ways in Khmer. It's as common as Smith is in the United States."

April 1998: Pol Pot dies in his sleep.

Sonn Senn sighed noticeably. "That is the history of Pol Pot's life—and death."

"Thank you for the recitation," Carter responded, "I am now more curious than ever."

"I was certain that you would be," Senn responded. "What is the nature of your curiosity?"

"That no one has come across any reliable evidence that Pol Pot is dead. The few pictures that the world saw in its newspapers could have been doctored. The so-called journalist who claimed to have viewed the body was known as more of a barfly than a writer."

"So you think that Pol Pot is not dead?" Sonn Senn smiled, knowing that he and Carter were now playing the mind game that they had played before.

"It really doesn't matter what I think, does it?" Carter asked, with a wry smile on his face. "You know what's on my mind right now, and it's why those officials who hired me to do a job wanted me to make sure he was dead." Pol Pot's crimes seemed the least of Carter's concerns about the man. Either he, Carter, was getting sloppy, as Atherton observed, or burned out, as Carter diagnosed himself to be. But if he was right, and Senn was not leading him down the proverbial garden path, then Carter needed more answers.

"You are a quick student, my friend," Senn interjected, "but perhaps an equally interesting question might be how Pol Pot could have entered your country, along with his murdering colleagues, considering that the quota for Cambodian immigrants is extremely small?"

Carter chuckled at Senn's use of "my friend." Yet, he believed him. "I suspect that one of us has the answers," Carter said, "and it certainly is not me."

33

QUEENS, NEW YORK

When they reached the end of the long corridor, Senn ushered Carter into a room in which small groups of Cambodians were either squatting on the floor in their traditional position or sitting on chairs. At the far end of the room was a large, rectangular wooden table. When they walked into the room and took seats at the table, everyone stopped talking.

Cambodians of all ages were present. Some were more elegantly dressed than others, but for the most part, they looked like working-class Americans. The teenagers wore jeans and had the usual paraphernalia hanging from chains around their necks.

The middle-aged women wore slacks and dresses. Only the elderly Cambodians wore remnants of their homeland—peasant shirts, beltless pants, bamboo sandals. Clearly, everyone was waiting for Sonn Senn.

"I think that you will find this very interesting," Senn said to Carter as he picked up folders from the table and scanned them. Carter was busy doing his own scanning, staring at frightened faces around the room.

"I suppose this is going to be some type of tribunal," Carter offered.

"As usual, you are quite observant," Senn responded. "Every month we have a meeting such as this. The people you see here represent members of the Cambodian community from all over New York City, and sometimes from as far away as Washington, D.C."

"And I gather that you are the judge and jury, all in one," Carter responded.

"Those are Western concepts," Senn responded. "I prefer to call myself the wise man of the village."

"Then you are even more elevated in status than I had thought." Carter noticed that the expression on the faces of the Cambodians he was watching in front of him took on a new look. Would it be called bewilderment? Before he could think about the look's meaning, an arm was thrust around his neck from behind. "What the hell is going on?" He was unable to turn around to see who held him hostage.

"I informed you previously that you must expect

all types of unusual occurrences in the Cambodian community."

Senn bowed, but not to Carter. To his strangler. "You are quite fortunate, Dr. Carter," Senn said.

Carter struggled to remove the arm that tightened around his neck, but to no avail.

"Take it easy, old chap." A familiar voice. "I asked you only last week if you were losing your edge," Atherton continued. "Now I'm really worried." He released Carter and helped him straighten up his clothes. Then the two men hugged.

"Welcome, General Atherton," Senn interjected, bowing again. He pointed to the seat next to Carter's. "Please make yourself at home. As you usually do."

Carter didn't know whether to be grateful Atherton was there, or knock him off his chair. He settled for receiving more information. "What does he mean by 'as you usually do'?"

"Let's just say that I have been here numerous times for different occasions," Atherton responded.

"To fulfill assignments?" Carter asked the question but did not expect to believe the answer. As Hamlet had said, "Something is rotten in the state of Denmark." Was Atherton a friend? Or a foe?

"Not always," Atherton responded. "I have been invited by Mr. Senn and other members of the Cambodian community to attend weddings, funerals, holidays . . ."

"Is there going to be a wedding here that I don't know about?" Carter's tone of voice was sarcastic.

As far as he knew, Atherton might have been sent there to complete the task Carter never did—kill Sonn Senn if he were Pol Pot. And maybe even kill Carter as well. Just like CIA agents, former assassins never just fade away. . . .

Senn watched Carter and Atherton's interchange. He had been told by Atherton that his relationship with Carter had been mentor-student as much as it had been employer-employee. He hoped that he and Atherton's little surprise had not changed that in any way.

As far as Sonn Senn was concerned, Atherton was one of many gray, amorphous creatures that slinked throughout the federal bureaucracy, keeping his hand, as the Americans said, in a host of people and events. He respected Atherton for what he was—a clever intelligence analyst who could have someone killed. That was real power. Senn knew that Atherton didn't need or have a fancy title. He worked in simple surroundings, many times out of a fast-food restaurant. But Atherton was Asian in the way he worked, like the Chinese triads, or the Japanese yakuza, or the Vietnamese gangs. If they did not bother you, it meant that you were not sufficiently important. Senn had great respect for the "interstitial man," the person who no one heard about, but was everywhere and potentially lethal. That was Atherton.

Atherton leaned closer to both Carter and Senn. "I came to inform both of you that you are in danger. Some of my colleagues think that documents

exist that would implicate them in—troublesome
events, let us say."

"If you do not mind my asking," Senn said,
"how did you find out this information?"

"Let me answer by saying that I have been employed to retrieve those documents, any way I can."

Both Senn and Carter understood the implication
of what Atherton had just said. Atherton had been
tasked to kill them both, but only after he found
what was wanted.

34

Senn showed no signs of disturbance upon hearing of Atherton's assignment. He turned toward the Cambodians in the room, motioned an elderly Cambodian couple forward, and began as he usually did. "What may I do for you?" he asked in Khmer.

"We came to America two years ago," the frail old man said, holding his wife's hand tightly, "and we have not been able to live very well."

Atherton translated for Carter.

"Do you have a place to live?" Senn asked in a quiet, gentle voice. "Do you have enough food, medicine, and clothing?" He could see that whoever had sponsored their arrival to the United States had been extremely negligent.

"We are proud people, Your Excellency—"

"Please don't call me Your Excellency," Senn interrupted. "I am Mr. Senn. I am not an imperialist or monarch. Just an ordinary citizen like yourselves."

Carter was impressed with Senn's humility, but couldn't help but wonder if this was merely a show for him. When he asked Atherton whether this was for their benefit, he was assured that what they were witnessing was real. That was why Senn was so popular among his own people.

"Thank you." The couple bowed in respect.

"Do you have children here?" Senn asked.

"He is over there!" The old man pointed his slim, frail hand toward one robust young man.

"Please come forward!" Senn's voice became noticeably more brusque.

"Yes, sir!" A rotund young man in his late twenties, with a hint of arrogance and defiance in his gait, sauntered to his parents' side.

Carter turned inquisitively toward Atherton, who merely nodded toward Senn as if to say, just wait and see.

"Your parents are complaining in a very indirect manner that you are not taking very good care of them," Senn began. "Are they correct?" He spoke in English.

"No!" The son responded in English, but

couldn't disguise in his voice the amusement he felt.

"Is there something that you find funny?"

"This entire procedure," the son responded. "We're in America, not Cambodia."

"What does that mean to you?"

"It means that I came here to this room, to see you, old man, because they begged me to. Otherwise, I don't go in for any of this Old World crap! And now I'm leaving you all to relive your memories." As the son turned to leave, two of Senn's bodyguards stood at each side of him and pushed him back to where his parents stood.

"Hey, what is this? I'm an American citizen. You can't do this. Not here in Queens. You may be able to throw your weight around in Cambodia, but here I can do whatever I please without some old man . . ."

He struggled to free himself from the bodyguards' grasp but to no avail. Senn rose from his chair and walked around the table to where the couple and their son stood. Without any warning he folded his second and third knuckles together and jammed them into the young man's larynx.

"U . . . g . . . g . . . g . . . g . . . g . . . h . . . h . . . h . . . h . . . !" The son fell to the ground.

"Take the boy's business away from him," Senn said to his bodyguards. "All the cash in the register and any owed to him will be given to his parents. If there is not enough money for them to live, then place the parents in the Cambodian Care House.

The boy will receive a weekly allowance for his
work until a fair arrangement with his parents is
worked out."

The bodyguards nodded. The frail, somewhat
bewildered couple followed the body of their comatose son as it was dragged from the room.

"Next case, please!" Senn said very calmly, returning to his seat at the table. He glanced at Atherton and Carter for their reactions. Atherton was
nonplussed. He had seen this form of justice before.
But Carter's eyes were wide-open. Clearly, this was
new to him.

A large Afro-American man and a short Cambodian man stood before the table. Senn nodded toward the Afro-American, indicating that he wanted
him to speak first.

"My name is James Washington, Mr. Senn. I am
here because Mr. Sirik Matak, standing next to me,
cheated me in a business transaction."

"Why don't you file papers in the American civil
court?"

"I have tried, but found them to be impersonal
and ineffective. Everyone knows you to be a fair
man," he continued. "I have come to you because
my problem is with one of the members of your
community. Mr. Sirik Matak sold me an insurance
policy that said if I were injured on the job I would
be reimbursed for any money I lost while I was re-
cuperating."

"And what was the nature of your problem?"
Senn asked.

"I had a mild heart attack," the Afro-American man responded, "but I was not able to collect any money from my disability insurance. The policy Mr. Sirik Matak sold me stated that I would be reimbursed two hundred dollars for each day that I was not working. But he did not send me any checks."

"What did you do, Mr. Washington?" Senn took note of Sirik Matak's frightened expression.

"Every time I called Mr. Sirik Matak he said the check would be sent to me soon. He said that I should have more patience. That it takes a long time for the insurance company to react."

"How long has it been since you should have received your checks?"

Senn wrote something down on a piece of paper and passed it to Carter. It read, "How much should he be paid in compensation?" Carter wrote back "I don't know!" Senn smiled in response, as if to say, you'll soon know!

"I haven't been paid for over one year," Washington responded, concerned that the wise man was distracted by the strangers next to him.

"Mr. Sirik Matak, how much does Mr. Washington believe he is owed?"

"I think that he believes he is owed three thousand dollars," Sirik Matak responded, eager to speak, "but the insurance company claims that he is not owed anything."

"Why would the insurance company refuse to pay him?"

"They say that the heart attack was not related to his job. They claim that Mr. Washington had a pre-existing condition of hypertension which he did not inform them about when he took out the policy and which he refused to treat with medication. They feel that they don't owe him anything. I am only a poor man caught in the middle."

"Why did you tell Mr. Washington that the check would be coming?"

"Because I was trying to give him some hope, as slight as it might be, that he would eventually receive some money."

"How much did you have in mind that Mr. Washington would eventually receive?"

"Maybe five hundred dollars!"

"So you would cheat him out of two thousand five hundred dollars? A man who had trusted you to be his agent to help him in the time of need?"

"That's not exactly what the case is—"

"Did you or did you not receive a check from the insurance company for three thousand dollars?" Senn looked intensely at Sirik Matak. He knew that he was lying about the insurance company's stories. It was cheaper for a company to pay on a small claim than to be taken to court—and possibly lose a larger amount. Beads of sweat were forming on Sirik Matak's forehead. His right eye began to twitch. "Think carefully on the answer, Mr. Sirik Matak. Whatever you say or do to someone in business generally reflects on all Cambodians."

Carter also watched Sirik Matak closely. He

thought that if this inquisition were to continue much longer Sirik Matak would suffer a heart attack from sheer fright.

"Yes . . . I . . . did . . . !" Sirik Matak responded with complete fear.

"Please tell Mr. Washington how much you received from the insurance company!"

"I . . ." Sirik Matak started to gag. Senn signaled to one of his bodyguards to bring a wastepaper can over to the man, who vomited in it.

"Please answer my question," Sonn Senn ordered when Sirik Matak finished. "Make certain that the number you are about to express corresponds to the true number sent to you by the insurance company. I think I know the number." Senn wrote something down on a scrap of paper.

"Five thousand dollars!" Sirik Matak responded softly.

"Please speak louder."

"I received five thousand dollars from the insurance company." Sirik Matak's entire body was shaking as he spoke.

"Why did you lie to Mr. Washington?" Senn asked.

"I had so many debts. . . ."

"How much do you have in your bank account?"

"I am in bankruptcy . . . I have no money except the house I live in. . . ."

"Mr. Washington, what would you consider to be fair payment for all of your troubles?"

"I don't know, sir!" Washington was more

shaken than he thought he would be. Someone actually listened to him and believed him. Tears welled up in his eyes. "I just never believed he would do something like that to me. I leave it up to you. No one up to this time has been able to get this crook to admit that he stole my money. Not the police. Not the insurance company. Not even my own friends who threatened him. He just swore on his ancestors' graves that he had not received any money to pay me."

"How much is your house worth?" Senn asked a blanched Sirik Matak.

"What do you mean?"

"You understood me!"

"I think maybe thirty or forty thousand dollars!"

"You have one more chance to answer the question correctly!"

Carter realized that Senn never had any real number with which to confront Sirik Matak. It was all a psychological game. And Senn was one of the best players he had ever seen. Carter looked at Atherton, who simply smiled and wrote the word *justice* on a piece of paper.

"I was told by a Realtor . . ."

"Yes?"

". . . that it should be worth sixty thousand minus the mortgage of thirty thousand dollars."

"So your house, in which your family lives I presume, is worth thirty thousand to you. Is that right?"

"Please, sir, I have one wife, three daughters, two sons—"

"You had no feeling of remorse or compassion for your fellow man who had been ill. Not only that, you took it upon yourself to cheat him of what belonged to him."

"No, sir. . . . it . . . was . . . a . . . mistake . . . I . . . was . . . going . . . to . . . pay. . . ."

"Mr. Sirik Matak, you will draw up a piece of paper which will be translated into the proper language by our own lawyers."

"No . . . please . . . I . . . will . . . have . . . no . . . where . . . to . . . go . . ."

"You will make out the title to your house to Mr. Washington. You will vacate it immediately and find somewhere to live. Since you were willing to make your family's fortune by stealing, you will learn what the consequences of that stealing mean to you and your children and your children's children. If they grow up without the comfort of a house, then they will curse you for the rest of your life. That is for the sin of cheating a sick man."

The man stood, trembling. Carter was concerned. He whispered to Atherton, "Do you think that was fair?"

Atherton whispered back, "It's not over."

"For having lied to me, and for having shamed your community, you will receive the punishment that our ancestors have meted out for centuries."

The two bodyguards grabbed Sirik Matak and

placed his left hand flat on the table. One of them pulled out a small butcher's knife from the back of his belt, raised it up into the air, and brought it down with the force of a blacksmith hitting his anvil.

Sirik Matak fainted.

35

"Are you shocked, Dr. Carter?" Senn watched Carter's face blanch at the sight of Sirik Matak's hand being cut off. "He still has one hand with which to make a living for his family. And now his family will be forced to work harder as well. It is a lesson for the entire community."

Carter had certainly seen and participated in torture and murder over the last twenty years, but there was something so cold and surgical about Senn's decision . . . one that Pol Pot could have made. . . . The justification seemed weak in comparison.

"Get the color back into your face, old boy."

Atherton whispered, "It gives us a very poor image in front of these people. They will think that we Americans are soft . . . or skittish . . . or . . ."

"Despite the fact that we bombed the shit out of their country," Carter whispered back.

"What I have shown you both is a glimpse of how a typical wise man of a Cambodian village would handle everyday problems." Senn knew very well that it seemed brutal to the Americans. "It is expected of me," he continued, in an attempt to soften his image in their eyes.

"Your justice system seems very similar to the Muslims," Carter noted. "If you commit a robbery, they cut off your hands. If you commit adultery, it's your neck."

"You are right, Dr. Carter," Senn replied. "Yet, you Americans consider the very same act that I just ordered to be a matter-of-fact part of Muslim culture. But, in the case of Khmer justice—"

"You mean, Pol Pot-style justice, don't you?" Atherton interjected.

Senn glared at the general. "As I was saying, justice by the Khmer is considered by Westerners to be cruel and unusual torture, befitting an international tribunal, for its condemnation. Don't you find that Americans are employing a double standard when indicting the Cambodian culture, but not the Muslim?"

"The death of a million or more Cambodians is not exactly comparable to utilizing a double standard. It's pretty forthright!" Carter responded more passionately then he had intended. Atherton gave him a stern look, warning him that he was walking down a dangerous path.

"Ah, Dr. Carter, should we then discuss the number of atrocities committed by the West?" Senn asked with sarcasm. Carter realized that he had just gotten himself to a place that he didn't want to go. He knew quite well the litany of atrocities to which there was no defense, let alone an answer.

"Despite our differing approaches to analyzing the past," Atherton said, trying to play the role of dispassionate mediator, "we do have a common purpose right now. Senn, when you called me to join you two you said that you had documents that would be of extreme interest to our government . . ." Atherton knew that Senn was talking about documents that were only reputed to exist, which would contain incriminating evidence against American officials both currently and previously in high office. And if Atherton knew this, other intelligence sources knew it as well. Which meant that the powers that be would soon be tracking his and Carter's whereabouts in order to get hold of the documents themselves. Time was a commodity that none of them could afford to waste on a discussion of comparative justice—or comparative evil.

"Thank you, General, for reminding us of our mutual concerns, but indulge an old man. I assure that we will have enough time. A discussion of evil, however, is never wasted, for even if you catch

Brother One today—or should I say Pol Pot—another one will arise, somewhere else, at some other
time . . . whether in the name of Islamic fundamen-
talism or in the name of democracy in Africa."

Atherton nodded his head in acquiescence. He
was here at Senn's good offices, which meant that
his time was now controlled by Senn's good
wishes. And he was aware of Senn's special relationship with Tom Reed—and perhaps others in the
administration—that probably gave him a false
sense of security.

"Your famous pilgrims came to America to seek
freedom of worship, did they not?" Senn continued.
"What did they do after they arrived?"

"They asked for help from the Indians and then
slaughtered them," Carter answered, knowing he
had been trapped in an intellectual cage of political
correctness and hoping it would be opened without
too much bloodshed. And without too much time
spent. The best thing to do was go along with Senn.

"But this American atrocity was covered, I believe, with a clever myth and an artificial holiday
called 'Thanksgiving,' was it not? The genocide
which the American settlers committed against the
Indians does not play a large part in American history." He paused, but received no response. "I am a
great student of American Indian history. I learned
a great deal about the dislocation and subsequent
death of your indigenous population from starvation, disease, and murder when they were forcibly
moved from their fertile land in the east to barren

country in the west, where there was no ability to grow food or hunt animals. Many scholars have compared the atrocities of Brother One in the long march to your Trail of Tears."

Carter continued to say nothing. He knew enough about American history to appreciate the similarities. But for the first time he realized how the atrocities committed in the name of civilizing America were perceived by another culture. And he felt defensive. Senn was right in saying that for every Brother One who Carter personally eliminated, another one would rise to take his place. Perhaps that was what Carter had been feeling for so long—the futility of it all.

"And how did Brother One come upon his ideology of building a new society by eliminating all traces of Western civilization from Cambodia?" Senn continued gleefully.

"His concept of starting with 'zero civilization' came directly from his intensive studies in France," Carter answered, wondering why Senn felt the need to continue this discussion. Okay, America isn't perfect. But at least we're always trying to get better. To live up to our ideals. "That still doesn't justify his actions."

"And your beloved Judeo-Christian religion does?" Senn asked rhetorically. "An ideology that justifies the exclusion of nonbelievers. With stories that fill the Old and New Testaments with murder, betrayal, deceit, incest. . . . And think of the terrible consequences that have resulted from your reli-

gions. Since before the time of the Crusades people
have died because they did not accept a particular
religious ideology, be it a so-called pagan who
slaughtered a monotheist, or a Christian who
slaughtered a Muslim, or a Muslim who slaughtered those who did not want to accept Islam as the
basis of their own belief system. And we all know
that it continues today."

"I think that you've made your point!" Atherton
said brusquely. "May I remind you that we are all
experienced adults. We are not in a university
course Religion 101. Quite frankly, if we don't go
about our intended business we should start a
course called Survival 101."

"I have to agree with General Atherton," Carter
interjected. "Time is going by and we have only
your word about the existence of incriminating documents. . . ."

"Incriminating documents?" Senn repeated the
words with a sarcastic edge. "How much more incriminating could the devastation of Vietnam and
Cambodia have been with your country's merciless,
round-the-clock bombing from twenty-five thousand feet in the sky? No 'documents' were needed
for that. No reprimand or discussion of evil acts
committed against my country. Perhaps there were
really two Brother Ones. Together they killed without mercy, compassion, or concern."

Both Carter and Atherton knew that Senn could
not be stopped or placated in any way. He had to let

the buildup of poison out of his system. But after that, what would he do?

"Millions of Americans believed that an ideology called Communism would infest the very infrastructure of your nation, some sixteen thousand miles away from my country." Senn spoke with a rapidity that revealed his excited state. "Why were they not condemned as war criminals? They committed the same atrocities as Brother One, except they used war machines which dehumanized the act of killing—bombers, tanks, flamethrowers, napalm bombs, Agent Orange. Your President Nixon was no less a war criminal than was Brother One. . . ."

Before Senn finished, one of his bodyguards walked over to the table and whispered something into his ear in Khmer. Senn nodded his head and turned toward Carter and Atherton.

"Please excuse me," Senn said in a controlled voice, "I have talked much. But as you can see, I feel quite strongly about the concept of evil. What it is. Who commits it. And most importantly, who decides who is evil and who is not evil." He paused. "My assistant informs me that your concerns about time have become increasingly more real. I think it is time to show you the documents that will insure our completion in Survival 101."

36

"What do you mean you can't find either Atherton or Carter?" Richards asked Reed, as they sat in his office. Winthrop stood looking out the window, disgusted with what he had been hearing for the last few minutes. Total ineptness, from all sides. Like most effective, wealthy businessmen, he was a pragmatist concerned only about maintaining the necessary environment for successful business. Recriminations and finger-pointing rarely inspired confidence. To ultimately come out winning, he had to maintain good relationships with everybody, even people he didn't respect. The businessmen he represented on the Business Council were only concerned with one thing—that the government didn't interfere with either their making or retaining money.

"I tried Atherton's usual hangouts," Reed responded defensively, "but I couldn't find him."

"So how do you know whether Atherton joined Carter?" Winthrop turned to them, exasperated. He was a businessman who represented hundreds of other businessmen who had billions of dollars at stake in the outcome of this discussion.

"I don't," Reed responded. He looked at Winthrop, in his expensive black silk suit, black shirt, and black tie, which might be fashionable by Hollywood standards, but was definitely not appreciated on the seventh floor of State. What really galled Reed was that Winthrop knew it but did not care. "When I last talked to him"—Reed turned to Richards, indicating in his quiet way that he didn't answer to Winthrop—"Atherton assured me that he knew where Carter was and that he was heading there. But he didn't give me any specifics."

Richards paced about the office, trying to figure out how to regain hold of a potentially disastrous situation.

"Don't you think it would have been prudent to have—"

"Gentlemen," Winthrop interrupted, "before we continue this useless finger-pointing, which serves no purpose at this time, may I remind you why I am here? And what you are here to do? You may not be as concerned about the president losing the election as I think you should be, but I'll be damned if I let anyone or any documents that may be floating around fuck with the work permits we need for the cheap labor we've been bringing over from Cambodia."

"Let's get this straight, Winthrop," Richards retorted angrily, "the reelection of the president of the United States is foremost on our agenda. We know that the presence of Cambodian refugees, whether they are Khmer Rouge or not, enables your people to function at a very high level of proficiency and effectiveness, for an extremely cheap cost. But it only works if we all work together." Richards was pissed off at Winthrop's patronizing tone. But he was even angrier at being reminded that no matter how fancy or prestigious his title, like all other secretaries of state, he served one primary function—to provide the vehicle beneath which American business could maintain its competitive edge in the world markets. The business of America was business. And Winthrop was here to make it very clear that despite America's ideals of democracy and humanitarianism, every secretary of state is beholden to America's corporate interests. And money.

"Mr. Winthrop," Reed added, deeming that the time was right, "there is no need to remind us of our primary purpose. Nor do we have to be hit over the head with your voracious need for cheap Cambodian labor . . ."

"Please, don't lecture me, Mr. Reed!" Winthrop

was definitely losing patience with these State Department cookie-pushers.

"I have no intention of lecturing you . . ." Reed replied.

"Then what are you prepared to do?" Winthrop interrupted, as if he were talking to one of his lowest employees. He was tempted to yell out "you're fired" but he reminded himself that he wasn't in private industry and it was more probable for him to resurrect Lazarus than to fire an FSO.

"Relax, gentlemen. Before I asked you both to this meeting, I ordered the National Security Agency (NSA) at Fort Meade to do an electronic sweep of the New York City area. Satellite surveillance should be able to pick up their conversation by targeting their voices. That's how we'll find Atherton or Carter or both."

"Very smart, Richards," Winthrop decided to throw him a bone of appreciation. Winthrop had been in the military and knew what NSA did. He likened it to a large listening antenna that could eavesdrop on anyone, anywhere around the world.

"Was that necessary?" Reed was startled by the lengths Richards was willing to go to find Atherton and Carter. "I'm sure Atherton will call in good time."

"Time is what is running out," Richards responded. "The issue is bigger than Atherton . . . or Carter . . ." He wished he didn't have to say what he was about to say, but he always knew that Reed would have to be let into the loop sometime. "There are documents being . . . held . . . in the Cambodian community . . . which, if leaked to the press, would ruin the president's reelection plans, and Mr. Winthrop's future. Plus mine. And yours—"

"And you've just decided to tell me this," Reed interrupted, not really sure what to make of Richards's revelation. "I gather that you're telling me because you need to, not because you want to."

"I was hoping to protect you. . . ."

"Bullshit! Whatever these documents are about, you've now compromised me. You've made me part of your dirty little scheme, whether I like it or not. What you've done is very smart, as Winthrop says, but not very legal!"

"What does he mean?" Winthrop asked Richards.

"There is a law that specifies that NSA is to be used to eavesdrop only on the conversations of foreigners. Not Americans. Even if they are criminals. Not that we really care at this point in time. But I have committed a major felony for which we could all be imprisoned for many years."

"Let's worry about that after we find the documents," Winthrop responded.

"Just for the record," Reed interrupted, "I don't want to know what is in the documents."

"Understood. But you do need to know their importance; they indict every president, secretary of state, National Security Advisor, and Business Council advisor since the Khmer Rouge rose to power."

"Did you ever really need Atherton to have someone find and kill Pol Pot, or was it really always about the documents?" The words came tumbling out of Reed's mouth with a great sense of having been betrayed. He realized that he had achieved his highest level in the foreign service that he ever would—unless he could hold Richards hostage. He had always considered himself a reasonably good game player. But in order to continue in the game, and rise to a more powerful position, he'd have to become intimately involved with more shit than he wanted to. And it scared him.

"I can assure you that it started way before me," Richards said, having decided not to take the rap for decades of deceit. "The . . . system . . . suspected that Sonn Senn had obtained copies of classified records through illegal methods to insure his own safety in the United States. They documented why President Carter allowed the Thai generals to open up the borders so that Pol Pot and his Khmer Rouge minions could seek sanctuary in Thailand at the very point in the war that the Vietnamese were finally in a position to decimate him and his followers. That evidence alone would expose the hypocrisy in the system and indict the former president, the ostensible champion of human rights, as well as his key advisors. Pol Pot's capitalistic streak of running guns and ammunition in return for jade and lumber allowed everyone to prosper. The Khmer Rouge. The Thais. The French. The Singaporeans. The Malayasians. The Chinese. The Taiwanese. And the Americans, who saw an endless flow of cheap labor. The Thais were thrilled to have the Khmer Rouge allowed into the USA. They didn't want the Cambodians to compete with their own workers. And American businessmen were so enamored with the possibility of cheap labor that work permits and visas were handed out like candy during Halloween."

Richards paused and stared at his startled audience of two. He wondered whether Reed appreciated the fact that he was trying to protect Reed's job . . . in an indirect way, of course. "If those documents are uncovered by anyone else but us, I'll lose my job. Reed, you will be reassigned, if not fired. And you, John, with your extensive network of upstanding American businessmen, will be in jail for a very long time. Let's see, now. For running illegal sweatshops all the way from Massachusetts to California. For paying off the Immigration and Naturalization Agency. For bribing senior executives, including several presidents of the United States."

"Then let's get those documents!" Winthrop interrupted. He could see that Richards was on the verge of a breakdown. If he didn't work with him, his own professional life would be over. All of a sudden he could empathize with someone like Mark Rich, who had fled the country rather than risk going to jail for his sins.

Reed felt even sicker after Richards finished his "speech." He knew that the State Department had no intention of returning Pol Pot to Cambodia, if he was ever found. Malavy would get over the loss, and continue to govern—for good or for bad. But lose his own job? Being relocated to stamp visas— until he left "voluntarily"—was not how he intended to end his career.

The telephone rang. Richards listened. When he hung up he was smiling. "We've got Atherton, Carter and Sonn Senn located at a Cambodian community center in Queens. I'm going to send out DSA agents to arrest them for illegal possession of classified documents. And if they happen to get hurt, or killed, as they resist arrest . . ."

37

QUEENS, NEW YORK

"It's time for us to find the documents that you have been promising." Atherton spoke with a sense of urgency as he powered off his cellular telephone. "We've got approximately one half hour before the DSA shows up. The sec state located us through an NSA sweep. It's clear to everyone involved in the mission that no documents are to leave this building. And none of us alive, if possible."

"Then we have no time to lose," Senn interjected.

"Maybe we should just all leave now and come

back another day for the documents," Carter suggested.

"Forget it, Carter!" Atherton responded brusquely. "Those documents in our possession will be the only thing that guàrantees our lives. You know Richards! Do you think he'll let a little thing like our lives interfere with some future he has already planned for himself?"

"Point well taken."

"I think it would be a good idea," Atherton added, "if we all kept our conversation to a minimum. We are being tracked by electronics that can pick up the sound of a needle falling on the ground."

Senn motioned them to follow him through a doorway which led to a twisted narrow metal staircase. It opened into a windowless room with four computer stations equipped with telephones, scanners, digital cameras, and DSL lines running everywhere. The Cambodians seated in front of each computer ignored the presence of Senn and his guests. It was as if they had been instructed that no matter what happened, they were to continue working on their tasks.

Senn led Atherton and Carter over to an old six-foot high walk-in safe and opened it. He motioned to both Atherton and Carter to step inside.

"Holy shit!" Carter mouthed the words as Senn handed him old, stained folders stamped TOP SECRET, NO DIS/NO CON, EYES ONLY. This is the mother lode, Carter thought. The folder he held contained agreements between the USA and Cambodia, allowing senior Cambodian officials to enter the United States under the category "Political Asylum," even if they were suspected of being Khmer Rouge.

Senn showed both Atherton and Carter a folder marked "Unannounced Agreements—1991 Paris Conference on International Participation for Peace in Cambodia."

Carter quickly scanned the documents out of personal curiosity; he had attended that particular conference in his capacity as medical officer for State's delegation. The folder contained several Memoranda of Understanding between the U.S. and Singapore, Malaysia, Thailand, Taiwan, and China. He caught glimpses of promises of assistance through the Agency for International Development (AID) if Pol Pot was left unharmed. This was to appease China's interests. In return, the parties to this concession would receive sizeable sums of money, mounting into the billions.

Atherton tapped on his watch to get Carter's and Senn's attention and spread out his ten fingers in front of his face. Time was running out.

"I don't think that both of you could go through all of this material even if you had ten hours," Sonn Senn said in a low tone. "Yet you cannot leave this material here. Neither your secretary of state nor Mr. Reed will allow us to leave this building alive. Not with what you have seen."

"Have they always known that you have had

these documents?" Carter asked, wondering why they hadn't gone after them before.

"Perhaps your secretary of state, who is a political appointment, guessed, or was told, that they existed. And his superiors. But no one was ever certain. And no one knew where they might be located."

"Up till now," Carter interjected. "I bet they were a very effective insurance policy for you and your Khmer Rouge friends."

Senn nodded.

"So why now?" Carter asked.

"I think the elections in Cambodia changed the situation. It may be one big show for the media, but our new prime minister will do anything he can to put Pol Pot on trial; and we former Khmer Rouge, who want to fit into your country, will do anything we can to resist exposure. The balance is no longer there."

Atherton checked his watch again. He thought he heard the distant sounds of helicopters approaching.

"We must figure out a way to get these documents out of the building without their having to disappear." Carter looked around the room at the Cambodians working at the computers.

"What do you mean, Dr. Carter?" Senn was not sure that he understood what Carter meant.

"You have a good point, old boy." Atherton reverted back to his patronizing English manner whenever he became nervous. "It's like the Chinese often say, 'an enigma without a paradox.'"

"Well," Carter responded, "if they don't find any documents they will think we hid them; I can assure you that they will extract the truth from us. It won't be pretty."

The sound of helicopters became audible to everyone in the room.

"Well, gentlemen," Atherton said, "I calculate that from the time they land in the small park across the street to the time they break through the front door we might have . . . five minutes . . . ?"

"Is that all?" Carter asked.

"That's about it," Atherton responded calmly. "If we could stall them downstairs, we might extract another five, but that's all. You can't gain more time than the big and little hands moving around the face of the clock allow you to have."

"You want to make a bet!" Carter suddenly realized what he had to do.

"Senn, can you order your men to secure the front door for as long as possible?"

"Of course!" Senn spoke in Khmer to a man seated at one of the computers who then rushed out of the room. He spoke to the other three men in English, instructing them to follow any directions Carter might give.

"Three minutes to go, gentlemen. . . ." Atherton announced, as if he were the timekeeper at a swim meet.

The sound of several helicopters swirling nearby

became excruciatingly loud. Carter took as many documents from the safe as he could hold and motioned to both Senn and Atherton to do the same. Files in hand, they rushed over to the Cambodians at the computers.

On Carter's command, each programmer scanned each document handed to him.

38

QUEENS, NEW YORK

"Why is it taking so long?" Richards yelled his question to Reed, who was sitting next to the pilot. Before the complement of three helicopters set out from Fort Dix, New Jersey, Richards had named their mission "Brother One," advising the army that their assignment would answer the question of whether Pol Pot was alive. That had given it the *gravitas* to accede to Richards's emergency request.

"Sir, it's extremely difficult to land a Huey helicopter filled with men in an unprepared landing area." Reed turned around to see how Winthrop was doing, sitting in a cramped position alongside the whining secretary of state.

"We've been hovering a good ten minutes. All of the helicopters seem to be in a hold position," Richards continued.

"The NYPD are cordoning off the park to pedestrians. They will let us know when it is safe to land. These soldiers and DSA agents have had extensive training in rappelling off a helicopter while it's in motion."

"Can't you just shut up for the moment?" Winthrop asked brusquely. Richards had made himself an unpleasant partner for the entire trip from D.C.

"Please watch your tone of voice, John," Richards responded, aware that the pilot might hear everything being said. "I'm not used to being spoken to in that manner."

"Well, get used to it!" Winthrop threatened. He had concluded that this secretary of state was too much of a liability for the business community, despite the fact that in the beginning of Richards's term the Business Council had thought that he was weak enough for them to manipulate easily. Well, Winthrop thought, when the gods are cruel, they grant your wishes. But Richards wasn't worth the trouble.

"I think that we are about to land right now," Reed announced, continuously checking his watch.

Richards squeezed his large frame through the narrow door of the helicopter as soon as the door

opened. He took a few steps away from the station-
ary bird and felt as if the ground was moving under
him. "I feel dizzy."

"That's a natural feeling for some people who
have never been on a helicopter before," Reed explained as he and Winthrop followed right behind.

Reed held Richards back as he tried to walk toward the community center building. "Wait a few
minutes. You can't afford to be dizzy during this
operation. The snipers need a few minutes to secure
the perimeter of the building . . . including several
rooftops. We don't know what kind of force we
may encounter. Remember, Mr. Secretary, we are
dealing with Pol Pot and the Khmer Rouge."

"Enough said." Richards pouted. But something
told him that this whole operation was taking much
longer than it should. Was Reed purposefully
stretching out the time before they could enter the
building?

A DSA agent ran over to Richards. "We know
from listening to their conversation through ELINT
that Dr. Carter, General Atherton, and Sonn Senn
are all in the building. I promise you that no one
will leave this building without being taken into
custody."

"That's the first good news I've heard all day."
Richards finally felt the ground securely under both
of his feet. He was relieved. Reed was right.

"General Bob Krensky at your command, sir." A
tall, handsome brigadier general saluted his secretary of state. "We have secured the perimeter of the

building. We've evacuated the surrounding buildings. Our snipers are in position. The NYPD will
provide backup support if we need to ram the front
doors. Your DSA agents will make certain that
throughout the conflagration—"

"Conflagration?" Richards interrupted. "What
do you expect in terms of opposition?"

"We have to be prepared for the worst." Krensky
responded with military curtness. "We're dealing
with a known group of men who are professional
assassins and another group who may have killed
thousands of their own people. I'm taking no
chances with you or with my men." Krensky looked
at a secretary of state who was clearly in awe of
him, and he loved it. "Just precautions, sir! I feel
confident that once you give us the word to proceed
we will be able to extract the opposition from the
building with as little collateral damage as possible."

"I do not want you or your men, or any people in
the building, to destroy any papers, documents,
disks, tapes . . ." Richards ordered. "Is that understood?"

"Absolutely, sir," Krensky responded with a
sharp salute. "Mr. Reed already gave me those instructions!"

"What else did Mr. Reed tell you?"

"Nothing much more than what you just said."
As he walked a few steps away, he stopped suddenly and walked back to Richards. "There was one
more thing that Mr. Reed instructed me to do."

"What was that, General?"

"To make certain that no one harms the old Cambodian man named . . ."

". . . Sonn Senn?" Richards asked.

"Yes, sir! That was the gentleman's name!"

Richards surveyed the scene. It looked as if a major battle was about to commence in a two-block area of New York City. Everyone was in his place, guns drawn, or about to be. Only what Reed was up to remained a mystery.

39

"This is Brigadier General Bob Krensky of the United States Army informing Dr. Allison Carter, Brigadier General William Atherton, and Mr. Sonn Senn to throw down any weapons they may be carrying and leave the building immediately, hands over their heads." Krensky's voice through his bullhorn could be heard for blocks.

Military snipers and soldiers armed with M16s were splayed over every rooftop. Police squad cars were blocking off the streets in a four-block radius. A hook-and-ladder fire engine had an extended ladder all the way to the top of the building. Nothing was left to chance.

"If you refuse to evacuate the premises within the next thirty seconds we will assault the building," Krensky continued.

"Dammit!" Richards grabbed the bullhorn. "Atherton and Carter, this is S. H. Richards, your secretary of state. We know you are in the building. Stop playing games. We want you to come out. We do not want any bloodshed."

"What about Sonn Senn?" Reed asked Richards.

"What about him?" Richards stood there impatiently. "You tell me!"

"There is nothing to tell." Reed tried to be reassuring.

"What are we waiting for?" Winthrop was pleased to see the army in charge. His opinion of the effectiveness of his two State Department colleagues couldn't be any lower.

"Isn't that a problem of *posse comitatus,* using military forces for a civilian action?" Even if it was, Winthrop was impressed by the power potential being held back all around him. Now that was discipline, he thought.

"We received a special exception from Justice because national security issues are involved," Reed responded.

"You have ten seconds to come out before we storm the building," Krensky shouted through the megaphone. He gave the signal to a unit of soldiers to approach the front and back entrances of the building with rams. The snipers signaled to him that they were on alert.

Before the building was touched in any way, the front doors opened.

"OK, stand down everyone," General Atherton yelled as he walked out of the building with both of his arms raised high up into the air.

Carter followed Atherton. "I'm coming out with Mr. Sonn Senn," he yelled out. Looking around, he was impressed by the armada that had gathered in such a short time.

Sonn Senn walked closely behind Carter, his arms raised slightly.

"That small Asian man behind Carter is more dangerous than he looks," Richards whispered to Krensky. "You have my permission to use lethal means anytime that you even think that he—or Carter—presents a threat to you or your men."

"Mr. Secretary," Krensky responded, "those are the broadest rules of engagement anyone has ever given me. Are you certain that you don't want to narrow the parameters?"

"No!" Richards responded vehemently. "You and your men have full discretion to shoot at will. Only General Atherton must not be harmed."

"Are Carter and the Asian spies?"

"Let's just say that Carter and Senn present a far greater threat to the United States security than you might ever imagine."

"General," Winthrop interrupted, "these men represent a new kind of warfare. There is no metal clashing against metal. It's not an enemy you would normally see through binoculars. It's economic warfare, where the enemy is largely, for the most part, faceless. But we are fortunate, this time, to have placed the faces with the acts of treason. And those two men Richards has pointed out to you may be the two most lethal enemies America has."

Richards looked at Winthrop with complete disgust. He wondered how he had never noticed just what a pompous ass Winthrop was.

"Yes, sir! I don't think that either of you will have to worry about their escaping . . ."

"In addition, General," Richards continued, "please make certain that the classified documents they stole and have in their possession are handed directly to me before any action is taken against them. Is that understood?"

"Yes, sir!" Krensky waved Carter, Atherton, and Senn over to a quiet area where they were immediately surrounded by military men and police. "Lay down on the ground with your hands and legs spread out. Don't make any movements whatsoever!"

"General Krensky," Atherton said from the ground, "you know who I am!"

"Yes, sir, I do!"

"Then stop acting like a horse's ass and listen to what I have to say before you go off like some dumb-fuck John Wayne!"

Even though they held the same rank, everyone in the army knew that Atherton could have been chairman of the joint chiefs of staff had he wanted to. Unofficially, he was senior to Krensky. Instead, he had gone off to create something that was very special and very dangerous, according to the military buzz. In fact, Atherton was a legend in the service. For Krensky, it was an honor to have met him. He found it hard to believe what the secretary of state had just told him.

"I can't sir!"

"What do you mean, you can't!" Atherton was angry enough to sit up, pushing aside the men who were trying to restrain him. "I'm your superior in seniority! I'm giving you a military order. No one can countermand that order. Not even the goddamn president of the United States! Do you understand me?"

Carter sat up as well. Maybe Atherton was finally going to exercise the power he always intimated to Carter that he had.

One of the more eager policemen began reading them their Miranda rights.

"I'm sorry we had to be so thuglike in our approach, but we had no other choice," Reed said to the group.

"Stop apologizing, Reed!" Richards shouted. "Where are the documents, Senn?"

"Which documents?" Carter responded.

"The ones that you and Senn stole!" Winthrop added.

"So this must be the business scumbag we've read all about!" Carter responded.

Winthrop smacked him across the face and Atherton had to physically restrain Carter from re- taliating. Richards couldn't look him in the eye. There are a lot of accounts to settle up, thought Carter. It was time for him to settle some injustices.

"Just tell us where the documents are that you stole," Richards said, "and I promise to do what- ever I can for you at your trial."

"Do you have a specific title or Dewey decimal number for what you are after?" Carter asked flip- pantly, wiping the blood from his nose that came from Winthrop's slap.

"Don't smart-ass me!" Richards screamed. "I'm your boss! I can have you charged with everything from treason to dereliction of duty, to espionage, let alone your other off-line activities. You won't see daylight ever again!"

Carter thought for a moment and then addressed Richards in a conciliatory manner. "Senn will go back into the building and tell his people to bring out the papers that these gentlemen are looking for, if that is all right with you."

"I'll accompany him," Reed offered. "Just to make certain that everything goes smoothly."

"That will be OK," Richards affirmed to Kren- sky, now certain that Reed and Senn had a special relationship. And it seemed that now was the time to ferret it out.

"Gentlemen," Carter spoke to both Krensky and Richards, "would you mind asking your patrol cars to turn on their radios to WSRP?"

"Very funny!" Richards responded. "You'll have enough time to listen to all the radio you want when you are in prison."

"I strongly suggest, General, that you do exactly what Dr. Carter asked," Atherton addressed Krensky.

After several minutes Senn and Reed emerged from the building, their arms laden with documents, accompanied by several policemen and several army officers. As they walked toward Carter, the sound of two gunshots was heard. Senn and Reed fell to the ground in a pool of blood.

40

Bring over the medics!" Carter was bent over Reed, whose head was covered with blood. "Set up an IV with plasma. He's barely alive." He had already ascertained that Senn was dead.

"Stop firing!" Krensky shouted through the megaphone as he ran toward the dying men.

"That's the smartest thing you've said all day," Atherton retorted as he ran alongside him. "Unfortunately, it's too late. Your 'snake-eaters' are quite good at what they do."

"Thank you, sir!" Krensky responded reflexively, then realized the faux pas that he had just made. "I'm sorry about what's happened. Someone had an itchy trigger finger and he'll be disciplined appropriately."

"It's not your fault!" Atherton responded, closing Sonn Senn's eyes. "Arrest our 'former' Secretary of State Richards and Mr. Winthrop."

"Upon whose orders?" Krensky asked.

"Who the hell do you think you are, General Atherton?" Richards asked indignantly.

"I am now your jailer, your nightmare, the worst living human being in your life, and I will continue to maintain that role until you rot in prison!"

"You're crazy!" Richards beckoned a DSA agent to gather the files.

Instead, two DSAs walked up to him, grabbed his arms behind his back, and handcuffed him. Then they did the same with Winthrop.

"What are you doing?" Richards shouted. "Release me immediately!"

"Sorry, Mr. Richards," Carter said coldly. "As of three minutes ago you were relieved of your position by the president. I expect that you will soon be indicted for a variety of felonious acts, pretty much the same ones of which you accused me. Isn't that a coincidence that we think alike."

"What do you mean?"

"The president of the United States has just issued a statement to the press, absolving himself from all knowledge of your illegal actions. However, I wouldn't be surprised if, in a few weeks, he resigned from his bid for reelection. For medical reasons, of course. It will be up to his successor and congress to decide whether to arrest him for crimes committed against the citizens of the United States and the country of Cambodia."

"Have you gone crazy?"

"If you had turned on the radio when I asked, you would have heard several of these documents being read aloud as a public service message. And the Internet went even faster. I can't begin to tell you how many millions of people are now reading the original documents that you signed with the Thai generals, which violated the Overseas Fair Practices Act with illegal Cambodian immigrants. And that's just the beginning." Carter turned to one of the policemen nearby. "I would advise you to read the Miranda rights to these men. There can be no technical problems with their prosecution."

He watched as Richards and Winthrop were pushed into a black SUV that sped away, sandwiched between police cars with flashing red lights and blaring sirens. The soldiers, police officers, and firemen began to disband. The helicopter pilots started preparing for takeoff.

When Carter rushed back to Reed, he was being strapped on to a gurney with an IV hanging from a metal pole. He stopped to look at the medic's chart. Fortunately, the bullet had grazed Reed's right temple but had not penetrated his skull.

"Thanks, Carter," Reed spoke slowly. His head was wrapped with blood-soaked bandages.

"You knew all along, didn't you?" Carter turned to Atherton.

"Knew what?" Atherton asked, stunned that Carter might know something that he didn't.

"Sorry guys," Reed continued, "but I'm the guy who started the whole thing."

"What's he talking about, Carter?" Atherton was almost flustered, a state in which he never allowed anyone to see him.

"If you look carefully at one of the documents you will see that it was Reed who made an agreement with the Cambodians, way before the agreement made by the sec state," Carter answered. "You see, General Atherton, Reed used both you and me brilliantly to create the image that Sonn Senn was Pol Pot."

"Wasn't he?" Atherton asked Reed.

"I don't really know. And I'm quite sure that no one will ever know who Pol Pot was . . . or is."

"But why would you want everyone to believe that Senn could be Pol Pot?" Atherton asked.

"So that the president of the United States, the secretary of state, and businessmen like Winthrop could continue their activities until someone like you, General, would call in someone like me, who would go from Boston to New York, chasing some ephemeral creation called Brother One."

Carter smiled at Reed affectionately. "This man knew that sooner or later I would find evidence that would incriminate the president, Richards, Winthrop . . . you name it."

"Why didn't you just . . ." Atherton stopped in mid-sentence realizing the question was ridiculous.

". . . go to the president?" Reed laughed. "There was no one to go to with documents that I could trust, short of the press. And even then, I wouldn't know which papers and journalists were beholden to the system."

"So Reed initiated a cat-and-mouse scenario," Carter continued for Reed, trying to save his energy, "that seemed to be of no threat to the president or the secretary of state. But he really set in motion a game in which the hunters became the hunted."

They watched Sonn Senn's body being transferred to an ambulance on the way to the morgue, where an autopsy was sure to follow. Who knows, thought Carter, perhaps in death we'll find out if he's Pol Pot.

"Don't think twice about him," Reed advised. "He was an old man who had committed his share of atrocities. He was persuaded by me to cooperate in this elaborate charade only by being threatened with deportation to Cambodia—as Pol Pot. We both knew that it really didn't matter to Prime Minister Malavy whether or not he was Pol Pot. Sonn Senn would have been slated as the star performer in the trial of the century."

As Reed was being wheeled away, Carter tore up a sheet of paper and threw it into the wind. "By the way, the document you signed years ago no longer exists."

"Thanks, Dr. Carter," Reed responded, as he was

lifted into the ambulance. "I'll probably see you as a patient in a few weeks!"

"You mean in a few months! That's my first prescription for you as your official State Department physician."

Carter and Atherton watched as the ambulance turned the corner, no longer in sight.

"Do you believe him that Sonn Senn wasn't Brother One?" Atherton asked.

"I believe what Sonn Senn said, that there will always be a Brother One, somewhere, sometime." Carter looked around at the neighborhood, as if searching for something. "I'm hungry. Let's go eat."

"Where?" Atherton asked.

"Any place that's open at this hour."

"You sure Sonn Senn wasn't Brother One?"

"If it makes you happy," Carter answered, "let's agree that he was. I'll even become Brother One if we don't eat right away, and you will be sorry you ever asked a question that should never have been asked in the first place."

"As you like." Atherton knew that Carter would never give him a straight answer to his question. Maybe that's why he admired him so much.

"But if Sonn Senn really was Brother One . . . then you would have hated yourself for the rest of your life."

"That's enough. Stop playing with my mind, Carter!"

"Then, feed me, Brother."

ABOUT THE AUTHOR

Alexander Court is a world-recognized "operational expert" who works on contract in a variety of overseas assignments. He has been a primary target for assassination by: Italy's notorious Red Brigade terrorist group; the former Soviet Union's KGB; the Cubans' Directorate General of Intelligence; the Cambodians' terrifying Khmer Rouge; and, the infamous General Noriega, who accused Court of "assassinating over two hundred people in Panama." Court's expertise includes the abilty to destabilize governments and conduct psychological warfare, using a panoply of methods to neutralize adversaries, be they individuals, groups, or countries. He has no known place of residence other than the location of his next assignment. *Active Pursuit* is the second novel in the Allison Carter, M.D., physician/assassin series. His first novel was *Active Measures*.